The Bird Is On the Wing

stories

The Bird Is On the Wing

Stories

Welton Rotz

TC Publishing
San Francisco

To Barbara,
Again, as always

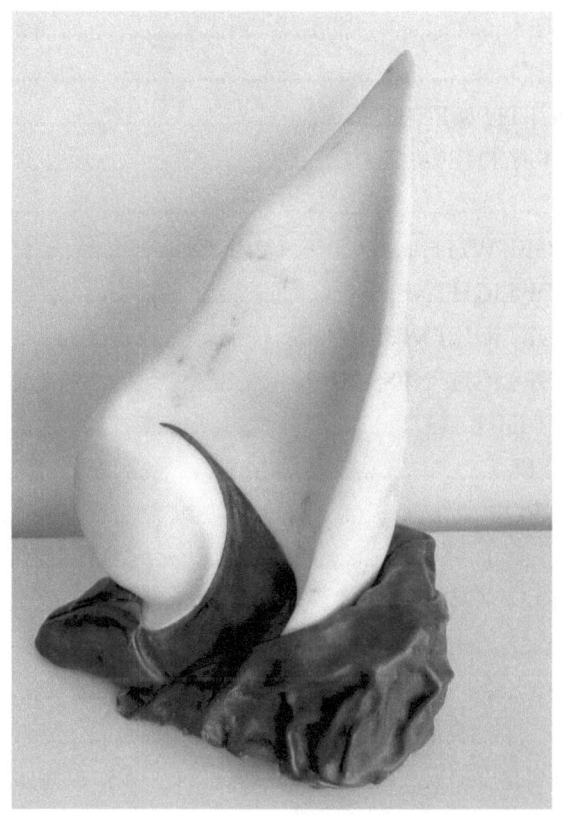

CONTENTS

iii

The Bird is On the Wing

"Come, fill the Cup, and in the Fire of Spring
Your Winter Garment of Repentance fling:
The Bird of Time has but a little way
To flutter — and Lo! the Bird is on the Wing."

— Omar Khayyam
Persian poet & astronomer, 1048 to 1131 CE

ABALONE

The hot mug of coffee and warm plate of pie feel good on my cold hands. I set them on the table and slide across the worn vinyl seat.

A voice says, "May I join you? All the other booths are full." An old man with a white beard like mine, also carrying coffee and pie, stands by my table.

"Of course," I say, even though I had hoped to have this time by myself, reminiscing about my life in Sausalito years ago. The weather is miserable, and the coffee shop, near the fish dock, had seemed the perfect place to pamper myself and my daydreams.

"Thanks. Name's Bill," he says, sliding into the seat opposite me.

"Pie's good here," I say. "What pie you got?"

"Apple. Can't say much for the coffee, though." Bill stirs sugar into the heavy mug.

Two old men sitting, talking about the weather, which is getting nastier. The coffee shop's clearing out, people off to work or whatever.

"You look familiar," Bill says. "Where have we met before?"

We explore possibilities, sailing, construction work, junior college classes, but no connection.

"I like your style," interrupts the waitress. "Dessert first. What can I get for you all?"

"I got a hunger for an abalone steak," says Bill.

"Not on your life, Dreamer. What's your second wish?"

Bill looks up at her with a big grin on his face.

"That's not on the menu," she says. "What's your third wish... for lunch?"

"I'll have a burger 'n fries."

"Me too," I say. "Make mine a cheeseburger."

After the waitress leaves, Bill comments on how attractive she is and adds, "If I were younger..."

"Yeah, right, about twenty-five years younger," I say.

We both laugh, remembering those times.

"Speaking of abalone," says Bill. "Have you ever gone diving for them?"

"A few times," I say. "Up along the Mendocino coast. We were free diving using snorkels. Air tanks and scuba were illegal."

"Why did you stop?"

I begin telling my story. How far it was to drive. Trying to find a diving buddy. The unpredictable water conditions, often rough or murky.

I stop and stare out the window at the Sausalito waterfront, my mind filled with those memories.

The waitress sets our orders on the table, pulling a bottle of ketchup from her apron pocket. It's a welcome break for me. My stomach is churning, and there's a bad taste in my mouth. Bill dives into his lunch. I take a sip of coffee...it's bad, bitter. I try some of my lunch. We eat in silence. It helps.

After a few minutes, Bill asks what happened up there.

"It's hard to talk about," I say, "Even though it happened a long time ago." With difficulty, I continue.

"The waves were breaking over the rocks farther out, but there was still a lot of surge where we were, in eight or nine feet of water. Visibility was hampered from silt and branches of kelp, so we stayed close together, maybe twelve feet apart. I needed to go up for air but saw my partner was thrashing about.

"Forcing my way through the current, I saw him struggling with his dive knife. Swimming closer, I could see he had the blade against his finger. The finger was clamped against a rock by an abalone. A wave broke overhead. The surge twisted his body, and he dropped the knife.

"I was out of air. I had to get to the surface. But so did my dive partner. I jammed my dive blade between the rock and the shell of the abalone and, remembering not to pry, twisted with both hands. The finger came free. My knife dropped, and with a hard shove I sent my buddy to the surface.

"Oh shit!" Bill mumbles through a bite of burger. "What was he thinking?"

"He told me when he came around the rock, there was a beautiful, huge ab. In his excitement, he dropped his pry tool, didn't have the wrist strap on. He needed air but was afraid he wouldn't find the prize again. So, since the abalone was standing well above the rock, he just grabbed it and pulled."

I feel sick to my stomach, reliving the horror of the last few minutes of the dive.

"So, the abalone lost; didn't get a finger," says Bill. "You know, when a group of ab divers get together, there's usually two or three fingers missing. You'd think people would learn."

We sit in silence, each with his own thoughts.

"I want to tell you something..." Bill says in a low voice. "Something I've never told anyone. I don't know the statute of limitations for this crime, but I think I'm okay." He begins, slowly at first, searching for the right words.

"The idea of being a commercial fisherman came to me in my mid twenties. Hanging out on the fish dock here in Sausalito, where many boats were tied, I met a fisherman named Hugh who was willing to take me on as crew because I knew about boating. I had a sailboat.

"We left the next morning, under the bridge, through the Golden Gate, and turned North, entering the Bonita small boat channel. Hugh, the fisherman, liked the way I handled the small boat. He told me to follow the channel, then head up the coast staying close to the Marin shore. Hugh went below to get some sleep. The boat was an old thirty-foot Monterey with the beautiful Clipper bow. Its rounded hull made it very seaworthy. I knew almost nothing about commercial fishing, but it did seem strange that there weren't any nets, crab pots, or even fishing tackle to be seen on board the boat.

"The ocean was very rough. The waves were so tall you couldn't see the channel markers unless we were both on a wave crest. I was thankful I didn't get seasick. Finally, we pulled into a sheltered cove. The cliffs above the rocky shoreline were very steep. No sign of a foot path down to the water. Hugh said it was the perfect spot, no recreational fishing. We dropped anchor just outside huge rocks with waves breaking over them.

"Once we were anchored, Hugh explained what we were fishing for. Abalone! Of course it was illegal, it was poaching. But there was good money to be made. The catch would be divided three ways; one for the boat's share, one for Hugh, and one for me.

Hugh would do the diving, gathering the abalone into getter bags. I would stay on the boat, tending the long air hose from the compressor down to Hugh, pull up the full bags, and dump the catch into the fish hold. I also had to make sure there were no loops or kinks in the air hose.

"'Most important. I'll make sure to watch for your air bubbles,' I said.

"Hugh laughed. 'Just watch the hose, Worrywart. If there's trouble I can drop my weight belt and come up for air.'

"Forty-five minutes after starting, Hugh came up and said we had to move in closer to shore to find more abs. I pulled up the anchor and let the boat drift in, right up to the rocks. The song of waves breaking nearby sounded like thunder.

"Hugh returned to diving for another hour. The boat's deck was rolling severely, making it difficult to pull up the bags. Hugh came up, saying he was tired and wanted to come aboard to rest. He was surprised to see the size of the catch in the fish hold. It must have been four or five hundred pounds, or more.

"'Let's go in,' he said. 'I think we have enough. Don't want to overload the boat.'

"I navigated the boat back to Sausalito while Hugh slept. He said we had a long drive ahead of us. It was almost dark by the time we tied up at the fish dock. Hugh drove his Econo Van out on the dock, right up to his boat. We transferred our catch, almost overloading the old van.

"Picking up some burgers 'n fries to go, we shared the driving to Monterey. Why Monterey? It's legal to fish for abalone down there, and the fish buyers don't ask questions. We arrived late at night, slept in the van until we could sell the catch in the morning.

"It was a long ride back to Sausalito. I wondered how much we had made from selling the catch. Hugh didn't even seem to know, but he was happy. Walking to my pickup, he counted out the cash. Almost five thousand dollars! My share of it was more than I could make in two weeks, or even three. And in just two long days! 'When can we go again?' I asked Hugh."

"That was a lot of cash," I say.

Bill smiles. "I need to take a piss," he says. "There's more if you're interested. And it gets better."

I think he's enjoying telling his story as much as I am listening.

Bill continues his story with the second time he went out with Hugh.

"We were giddy with anticipation after the great success from the first trip. However, we got off to a bad start. Hugh was late getting to the boat in Sausalito. Turned out his old van wouldn't start, so he took his wife's car, which caused a fight. We faced a flood tide, so it took longer to go through the Golden Gate and out to the ocean.

"Arriving at the dive site, we set the anchor and began preparing the equipment. Hugh had bought three new fifty-foot coils of water hose from a garden supply store. This would be his air line, to replace the single fifty-foot hose we had used before. He hoped, with the longer air hose, we wouldn't have to relocate the boat to a new dive site.

"I was apprehensive about using the water hose. It wasn't designed to carry air pressure. Also, the new hose hadn't been stretched out to release the coils; they could cause a kink in the air line. Hugh finally agreed to uncoil the 150 feet of hose even though it would take time from the dive.

"The air compressor ran off a drive pulley on the front of the boat's diesel engine. This worked well when the engine was at idle.

But when the boat was under way and the engine speeded up, the rubber belt driving the compressor had to be disconnected from the drive pulley. An easy enough job, but it required going below and creeping forward in the engine room.

"As we were rolled out the air hose, I realized the boat was drifting into the rocks and the anchor was dragging. Hugh ran to the controls, shouting to me to pull up the anchor. It came up easily, its flukes buried in a tangled ball of seaweed. We relocated to a new spot, not so close to the rocks. The anchor cleared, cleaned, and set.

"I gathered the air hose ready to feed it out to the diver. All the while I worried whether the compressor was powerful enough to pump air through 150 feet of water hose. Hugh wasn't concerned, he just wanted to start diving. Overweight with a big belly, he struggled to squeeze himself into his neoprene dive suit. Putting on the weight belt was next, all fifty pounds of lead attached to an old military ammunition belt which barely fit around Hugh's ample middle. He sucked up and with difficulty got the belt's hook and eyes to catch. I asked him how he could release and drop the weights if an emergency happened. Hugh just laughed, attached the air hose to his dive mask, and jumped overboard, sinking very fast with all the weight.

"I was busy playing out the air hose, making sure it didn't kink, and pulling up getter bags of catch. Gazing out over the water after stowing the second bag, I wondered if Hugh had reached the end of the air line. With a shock, I realized there weren't any air bubbles coming up.

"Oh, shit! I had to get Hugh up to the surface for air immediately.

"I glanced down into the engine room…the drive belt for the compressor was off. Decision! Creep down and reattach the belt to the compressor? But the belt might be damaged. Or the problem

7

may be a kink in the air line. Pulling on the air hose would not work. It might be damaged or wrapped around a rock. The water hose fittings were minimal and not meant to be pulled on. Both getter bags were up on deck. The only option left was the lightweight signal rope the diver used to call for a getter bag to be pulled up.

"I pulled gently, my mind racing. How fast and hard to pull? Too hard and the small rope might break. Too slow and Hugh might drown…if he was still alive.

"Slowly, hand over hand, I pulled up the line. Hugh's body appeared, underwater, not moving. The small rope was attached to his diver's belt. My heart pounding in my ears, I reached over the side of the boat and turned the body over so the face was above the surface. Hugh was hardly recognizable, his face so bloated and purple. How was I supposed to get him into the boat?

"The body moved, sounds came from the face. Hugh was alive!

"Somehow, to this day I have no idea how I got Hugh on deck.

"Then I got busy preparing to leave. I emptied the two getter bags into the fish hold. Only a dozen. I tied Hugh to the deck so he wouldn't roll overboard. I raised the anchor, letting 150 feet of hose trail out behind to work out the last kinks.

"Hugh was feeling sick. He threw up on the deck where he lay. I set the course south for home. I began shaking; a bad stomach taste filled my mouth. Too much adrenaline. I lost control of my bladder. Hugh slept all the way through the small boat channel. Passing under the Golden Gate Bridge, Hugh woke up, and struggled to unfasten the weight belt. It took both of us to get it off. I told Hugh that I wouldn't dive with him again until he had a new, quick-release weight belt.

"Arriving at the fish dock, Hugh was feeling better. Looking in the fish hold, he decided there were too few to drive to Monterey. He said we could sell them in Chinatown.

Parked on a side street in the heart of San Francisco's Chinatown, Hugh stood by his car with an abalone in his hand. Pedestrians stopped and asked, 'How much?' but didn't buy any, so Hugh began lowering the price. My job was to watch out for police, on foot or in patrol cars. Street selling was illegal without a permit. We were about ready to leave when another van pulled up and parked in front of us. They had puppy dogs for sale. Soon a small crowd gathered. The buyers were not petting the dogs, they were feeling the legs. We sold our catch to people accustomed to buying illegal sources of protein. It had been a long, tough day, a hard way to make twenty dollars."

Bill lifts his mug of coffee, puts it down and takes a sip of water. "So, that's the end of that chapter. There's more if you want."

"Oh yes!" I say. "It's fascinating. I can see why you understood when I told the story about my buddy's finger."

"Yep, been there, done that. I gotta take a leak, be right back. That's the trouble with getting old."

I think I see tears in his eyes before he wipes them with a napkin. Is it reliving the near drowning? Or what? The waitress comes over and clears the lunch dishes. I ask her if it's okay for us to sit here longer.

She studies the pelting rain out the window. "No more customers coming in on a day like this," she says. "Would you like dessert? We have one slice of pie left."

"Yes, please. Would you divide it on two plates?"

"Sure. Do you want to know the flavor?"

"Nope. You surprise me. It'll be good whatever."

Bill returns and continues his story.

"It was three weeks until I heard from Hugh. I'd been wondering if I ever would. Hugh said he had done a lot of work on the boat and dive equipment. Proudly, he announced the purchase of a new (to him) dive air hose, and a new weight belt. A week later we went out again at first light. The weather was good and the sea was calm.

"Arriving at the dive site, we made sure the anchor was well set. We checked out the new equipment, including a stronger signal rope, one that could pull him up if needed. Understandably, Hugh was in no hurry to dive. After checking the quick release on his weight belt, he jumped overboard. Before long, he sent up the first getter bag with a nice catch.

"I was just starting to dump the abalone in the fish hold when I heard gun shots. Looking up, I saw two men standing on the edge of the bluff above us. One had a rifle; the other was looking through binoculars. As I watched, the rifleman took aim and shot at us! I admit I was more frightened than I could imagine. He missed, but I could see the bullet hit the water near the boat with a loud 'shoop!' sound. Dropping the getter bag on the deck, I grabbed the new signal rope and pulled.

"Hugh came up, wondering what was going on. As I explained, another shot rang out, the bullet hitting the water even closer. 'Shoop!'

"Hugh came aboard, dropped his weight belt, air hose, and partly filled getter on the deck. I ran forward and pulled up the anchor. Hugh was in the pilot house trying to shift the engine from neutral into forward. The shift lever was stuck! The boat was drifting back into the rocks. Hugh hoisted himself up and kicked the shift lever with both feet. It broke! I felt spray from the waves breaking over the rock just next to us. Hugh dove into the engine room and with a pipe wrench forced the transmission into forward. We headed out to sea. Back on the bluff, the man with the rifle raised it in the air in triumph.

"Clearing the north end of our cove, we saw a vessel belching black diesel smoke coming at us full speed down the coast. Hugh swore, saying it was the Fish and Game boat. We couldn't outrun them. Slowing down, we released and swung out the long salmon fishing poles on each side of our boat. It looked like we were trolling for fish. Setting our engine speed, we headed out to sea away from the coastal abalone diving area. Much of our course took us out of sight in the troughs of waves. The Fish and Game boat passed behind us, continuing their search for abalone poachers along the shore. Hugh slipped out of his dive suit. We pulled in and stowed the air hose and getter bags we'd been towing. If we had come close to being apprehended, we could have cut everything loose. With no evidence on board, we would go free.

"We were both pretty down when we made it back to Sausalito. It was too late to take the few abalone we had to Chinatown. Hugh knew a bar near his home that bought and sold illegal items through their back door. He invited me to come along as lookout. Hugh was very paranoid after the close call. He said we could go to his home for supper after.

"His wife made us the most delicious omelet I have ever eaten. She called it the Abalone Diver's Omelet. Perfect for quick meals, since she never knew when Hugh would come home from fishing. I still make it for myself with eggs, browned onions, fresh green onions, chopped tomatoes, garlic croutons, ground sage, and lots of cheese.

"It was another three weeks before I heard from Hugh. He had a sure-fire idea for abalone diving. I told him I wasn't interested. Even with the delicious omelet, the ten dollars earned was not worth the day out there. Hugh convinced me to come to his place, hear him out, and enjoy another Diver's Omelet.

"Hugh's idea was simple. Since I lived in west Marin, I could drive out to the Seashore Headlands, set up, and watch for the Fish and Game boat. Hugh had acquired two ship-to-shore radio telephones. This was well before cell phones. They each came in a wooden crate, larger than a shoe box.

"We set up a date and time, mid-week. Less chance of Park Rangers. Hugh had another fisherman to crew on the dive boat. This meant the catch would be divided four ways, not three. But the potential was there."

Bill pauses, fidgeting with a cold French fry, then turns to me. "There's one more chapter…are you game?"

"Oh, yes!" I say, "I'm intrigued. What happened?"

A grim look crosses Bill's face. He takes a sip of tepid coffee.

"You okay?" I ask. You don't have—"

"No. I have to tell it out loud. It's very personal, and I've never told anyone. You're a good listener. So, here goes…" He takes a breath and begins.

"I drove out to the vast, uninhabited Headlands. Maneuvering my pickup off the road and hiding it behind some bushes, I carried the radio box, a small stool, binoculars, and a knapsack with food and water to the bluff above the ocean. It was near the spot the shooter had stood. In fact, I found some empty rifle shell casings. This was a good location to watch both up and down the coast.

"Hugh's boat was just coming into view. We made radio contact.

"'Are you there?'

"'Yes, are *you* there?'

"'Yes. Good view?'

"'The best?'

"That was the last radio contact.

"I watched the dive equipment being set-up below for a few minutes. Relocating a few yards back up the slope to a higher spot, I had a better coastal view all the way south to the Golden Gate, and to the north until the coast disappeared in the mist. I laughed, thinking of the phrase 'The coast is clear.' Hoped it would stay that way.

"The day was beautiful, sun shining with a gentle ocean breeze. My little bench was comfortable. I'd taken a beginning meditation class, had been uncomfortable sitting, so I'd built this portable bench. Facing the ocean gave me an easy view both up and down the coast.

"A deer slowly walked up to me. I sat very still. Coming closer, the deer cautiously stretched out her nose, touching my outstretched hand.

"'Why,' asked the deer, in a loud clear voice, 'Are you doing this?'

"I started to choke up, feeling the awe of the moment. I hugged myself. The deer and I looked into each other's eyes for a moment, lost in space and time. As the deer slowly moved away, nibbling on shoots of grass, I felt myself also moving.

"My body was changing, filling out, expanding. I could still see all the way up and down the coast. Everything was merging, shifting, unfolding. Everything blended into shades of blue, the sky and ocean, and the rocks and bushes. Everything became... everything. And one. I could no longer see my body. I was dissolved into the whole, I WAS the sky, the ocean, the rocks, the All. A feeling of joy surrounded me.

"The new feeling was accepted, not questioned. Time stood still. There would have been a grin on my face if I had a face. Images flashed through my mind, too fast to be held...to be questioned...

to be examined. I liked where I was. After an hour, a minute, or an eon, my body reemerged, sitting on my meditation bench. I wished I was a dancer...I'd dance. Or a singer...and sing. Or a poet, or an artist.

"I stood up, stretched, and walked down to the edge of the bluff. Hugh's boat was gone. Looking south, I thought I could just see a small gray fishing boat turning into the Golden Gate. The radio telephone didn't work. Maybe I'd left the power switch on and the battery was drained? Nope, still plenty of power. A storm was building out to sea. It was time to go home."

Having finished his story, Bill sits quietly across from me, hands folded on the table, head bent.

"That must've been awesome," I say.

He just nods.

I reach over and touch his hand. "Then what happened, or was that the end of the story?"

"I didn't hear from Hugh, and his home phone was no longer in service. Maybe he couldn't pay his phone bill. A month later, I drove to Hugh's place, taking the radio telephone. He was there, said he was sorry, no Diver's Omelet, the chickens weren't laying.

"I returned the telephone, saying that it hadn't worked. Hugh responded with a shrug, didn't seem to care. He'd left the dive site when there were no abalone to be found, and his radio didn't work either. When I asked if he was still diving, Hugh shrugged again. 'Nope.' I asked what happened.

"Returning from the dive, they tied up to the fish dock and left. The storm was just breaking. Somehow, that night, the boat broke loose and was driven under the dock. The rising tide and the storm waves smashed the boat. It sank. Hugh was not concerned. It wasn't his boat, he'd borrowed it. Since then, Hugh had been repairing VW bugs for hippie customers who had very little money."

"That's quite a story!" I say. "What about you?"

"Things worked out for me," Bill says. "I started meditating regularly. At first focusing on a deer, but then on a large disk of light."

The waitress clears the lunch dishes and leaves a bill. I put down some cash and head to the restroom in a hurry. I tell Bill I'll be right back.

It takes longer than expected. I don't like being an old man. Returning, the restaurant is filled with a glow; the storm has passed. Light streams in through the open door, so bright I have to blink. Bill is not at the table. There's just one coffee mug on the table and some change. I grab my jacket from the old vinyl seat and run to the door. Outside, it takes a minute for my eyes to adjust to the bright light.

Bill is nowhere to be seen.

DILL WEED

"UMMmm, That smells so good."

"Yes," says Barbara, "I know you like dill. I used fresh dill in the salad tonight."

"The smell brings back so many memories," I say.

I'm sitting on the tailgate of the farm wagon. My legs, hanging over the back, brush the tall weeds that grow between the ruts in the center of the dirt road. The tractor is moving slow enough that the slapping of the weeds on my jeans doesn't hurt. On one side of me is my ten-year-old big sister, on the other side is the teenage daughter of the relative we are staying with.

Following close behind my legs is a stirred-up cloud of insects and THAT SMELL! A smell I have only experienced from a distance, like being at the threshold to the real thing. My mother opening a jar of pickles, that smell, but mixed with the odor of vinegar.

Here I am, in the full thickness. I have arrived, completely wrapped in the pure fragrance.

"What's that wonderful smell?" I ask my companion.

"Oh," she says, "That's dill. It grows wild, it's everywhere. We use it when we jar up a batch of pickles."

I feel like jumping off and rolling in the wild dill.

My sister and I are staying with relatives in Pennsylvania for a few weeks in early summer before I start fourth grade. A new experience and new smells. I have already lived in five different homes with my family, each with its distinctive, identifying collection of odors. The intoxicating aroma of fresh rain on the hot, dry desert of Arizona. The cold, dry scent of new snow at night in upstate New York. In Illinois, rolling in a raked pile of leaves, and running through the smoke, getting a little dizzy, when the pile is set on fire. The stench of automobile exhaust in a crowded city when my parents studied Chinese at Yale University. On my mother's family farm in western Kansas, the pungent fragrance of working men. My grandpa and uncles, coming in for the noon meal, having washed up at the hand pump by the back door, still smelling of the mix of sweat, dust, and fuel on their bodies.

Dill weed is only the first of powerful memories of this visit to the farm in Pennsylvania. I can only remember one hard, fast rule on this farm: "Never go into the hog pen, don't even climb on the hog fence." We were told, "They are not pigs, they're hogs, huge hogs. They will kill and eat anyone that comes into their space. They're mean." The smell? Hog shit smells like human poop.

Chickens raised on the farm are prepared for market. On butchering day, my job is to carry the buckets of offal, the guts and heads, out to the hungry hogs. I dump them into the feed trough from outside the fence. The smells of the butchering, the blood, the wet feathers being removed, and my offal buckets all add up to my memory of the stench of death.

The farm also does custom slaughtering of larger animals. I watch when a neighbor farmer brings in an old cow, well past her time of breeding and milk production, to be put down. It takes three shots to the head from a .22 rifle for the cow to drop to her knees. Her throat is cut, she bleeds to death. The stench of her hot blood mixed with her release of poop stays vividly in my memory.

Every morning, after breakfast, I help with meal cleanup. The slop pail is pulled out from under the sink. The table scraps of uneaten biscuits and gravy, leftover pancakes, and unfinished glasses of milk are scraped into the pail. Eggshells and peelings from breakfast fruit are topped off with warm bacon fat from the heavy cast iron skillet. I enjoy delivering this treat out to the hogs. It is like carrying a bucket full of breakfast aroma.

After breakfast cleanup, we start preparing the next meal. Dinner is the midday meal, supper is after work in the evening, and lunch is a small meal taken out to the workmen in mid afternoon.

Pies are made and placed in the oven. Apple is my favorite, with its aromas of cinnamon, star anise, and spices. Beef stew with fresh carrots, onions, and potatoes from the garden simmers on the stove. Bay leaves are the only ingredient not from the farm. My sense of smell is almost overpowered by the cooking and baking.

My job is to ring the dinner bell to call in the men. The large, cast-iron instrument is activated by pulling on a rope attached to an arm, causing it to swing. The heavy clapper inside hits the rim. The iron bell emits a harsh clang, not the pleasant ring tones of bronze.

The dinner bell originated from the time when men didn't wear watches and needed to be called in for the meal. No call was necessary in the morning. The roosters, which were free to strut around the yard, made sure everyone knew when first light appeared.

Likewise, it was easy in the evening to tell when to come in…the sun was setting.

A few days before we leave, my sister and I help put up pickles from the first crop of ripe cucumbers. We pick a basket full, just the right size to fit in Mason jars. The kitchen is crowded with canning equipment and three women working around the table. I am too short to stand and work. My assignment: to walk up the dirt road and pick dill weed.

I know where the best dill grows. Up past the barn and the odor of chickens, well past the disgusting stench of the hog pen, out of sight of the slaughtering building and the memories, is my favorite patch of dill. Bending over, I cut sprigs with my pocketknife. By this time in my life, I am carrying a knife as an important accessory to my daily dress. When I finish gathering the herb, my hands are covered with the sap of the plants. I can taste as well as smell the aroma.

My final memory of that month spent on a farm in Pennsylvania is laying down in the middle of the road, between the ruts, rolling over and over, becoming totally saturated in Dill Weed.

THE FOURTH & FIFTH

When the Sphinx, in Greek mythology, asked, "What goes on four feet in the morning, two feet in midday, and three feet in the evening?" Oedipus answered, "A man in childhood would go on hands and knees (four feet), during adulthood would walk on two feet, and in the evening of old age would make use of a cane or staff as a third foot to touch the earth."

Little did the Sphinx know that there is a fourth way for a human to "go," touching the earth.

Wheels.

I was maneuvering about on earth in the evening of my life, using a trekking pole "third foot" when I fell, and fell hard. It was in my doctor's office, no less.

"It's time," she said, "to move on to a walker."

I became an old man, head bent, shuffling along with a two-wheel walker. You know the kind, two small wheels in the front with tennis balls on the back legs so it will glide easier.

It's hard being an old man. The image of shuffling does not fit my self-image. Is this a time beyond the "evening" in my life? Now what?

The discovery of a four-wheeled walker gave me a new perspective on life. It had hand brakes, a seat, and could fold. Best of all, it fit in the trunk of my car. I would creep along the side of the car and slide into the driver's seat. Hand controls for throttle and brake freed me to drive anywhere.

Anywhere, until my legs completely gave out and my eyes became undependable. Giving up driving was just another activity that had to be relinquished along with the four-wheeled walker.

Next, a wheelchair.

It's comfortable, and I can maneuver around the apartment by myself, making breakfast, etc. But I need assistance when I go out. So, I do not leave the apartment very often.

If depending on wheels is beyond the time of "going on three feet in the evening of a man's life," and a walker or wheelchair moves in and becomes the fourth way to touch or step on the earth, what's next?

Perhaps it is time to fly, to lift the feet off the ground. This seems to have been outside the awareness of the Sphinx. To go past the evening time of a man's life, to venture beyond even the fourth way. Perhaps there is a fifth state when man lifts off the ground. When he is no longer standing on four, two, or three feet. Or even using wheels to touch the earth, it is a time to flutter.

Omar Khayyam, the Persian poet and astronomer who lived from 1048 to 1131 CE, wrote this poem, which speaks to me:

The Bird is On the Wing

"Come, fill the Cup, and in the Fire of Spring
Your Winter Garment of Repentance fling:
The Bird of Time has but a little way
To flutter — and Lo! the Bird is on the Wing."
— Omar Khayyam

This is no longer the evening time of life. No longer the added years of limited mobility with the use of wheels. This is Spring! A time of new life, new ways. A time to fling away a lifetime of…of… well, of life.

Giving in. Giving away. Giving up. Letting go. Letting in.

And what is next? A bird can flutter for only so long. And the bird is on the wing.

We have been given the awareness. Are we ready?

It's exciting, and downright frightening, to think, to imagine what that fifth state

        may be,

                can be,

                        will be.

The Bird is on the Wing
Sierra White granite
10 ft. by 4.5 ft. x 1.5 ft.

FLIGHT FEATHERS

Something is happening
all too fast
Yesterday, I lost a feather
It was a flight feather
Today, I lost two more
Yesterday, I tried to glue it back on
It would not stick
Today, I tried to pick them up
They kept slipping out of my hands

This is no mid-life molt

Some day (or night)
I will fly again. I'll not need feathers
With a hop, and a skip, and a grin on my face
I'll speed to what Ram Das calls
The greatest adventure of all,
that is why it is saved to last.

CARNOC

"MMOOooooo" Comes the greeting from the stone.

Rounding the tall megalith, both the cow and I are startled. The place is deserted, except for us, the wind making a gentle rustle in the grass. The cow lowers her head and continues to eat. Around me, extending for more than a mile, are rows of quiet, ancient standing stones.

This is Carnoc, on the west coast of France. Not well known at the time, usually only a footnote in articles about Stonehenge across the Channel in England. Here, the stones are not as large, but are spread out over a larger area. Some are in rows that march across the road. Continuing through the small village, like quiet sentinels standing guard, oblivious to the passage of time. Time not measured in years, but in centuries, even back to myths and fairy tales. What are they guarding? What secrets are locked within their rough, lichen covered exteriors?

Walking along, passing stone after stone, crossing to another row, I am drawn to the center. This is the beginning, the origin of the rows marching out from the core. At the nucleus is a stone table. Were offerings placed on its flat surface? Were they blood sacrifices? I see no groves or channels for blood flow carved in the alter. Relieved, I scramble up and lay down on the sun-warmed hard surface. With my jacket as a pillow, I relax.

Thoughts and images rush through my mind. Perhaps I drift into a deep sleep, listening to the sounds of the wind. The sounds change. My scattered thoughts draw into focus, or maybe I awaken. Along with the rustle of the grass, the wind carries sounds of music. It is hauntingly beautiful. Sitting up, I hang my legs over the edge. In the distance, a group of people are coming. All are women or children. Some are playing instruments; lap harps, pan pipes, and flutes. There is movement, some are swaying, dancing. No one appears to be in a hurry. They slowly weave in and around the ancient stones. Coming closer.

Boom, thuk, thuk, boom, thuk, thuk, Boom...thuk, Boom, ..Boom

The sound of drums in the distance approachs from the ocean or the shore. The two strains blend, giving a rhythmic beat to the flowing, ethereal notes from the women's instruments. The music touches my core, my very being. I watch and listen, feeling the music in my chest and in my gut. Soon, the men appear. Slipping over the edge of the altar, I join them as the two groups meet. No one seems to notice me, even though my jeans and flannel shirt are very different from their simple homespun attire.

No rushing together, no dashing. Each group moving slowly, cautiously approaching the other. I can feel the overwhelming emotions transmitting from both groups. Even the small children press against their mothers' legs. Fear, anticipation, and excitement are all tumbling together within both groups. I am caught up in the feelings, a part of the gathering. And yet, I am separate, apart, an observer.

A man and a woman meet. The music and the dance continue. The couple's eyes meet as they circle each other. Is this my mate? It's been a long time, too long. Memories have faded. The men ask another question: is this my child, no longer a baby? If there is no spark of recognition between them, each moves on to find another.

When a couple is joined, they move away to the altar. New emotions saturate the air…relief, joy, and love.

The music thins out as the musicians find their mates. The drumbeat intensifies. A feeling of desperation pervades the remaining few. Partners have died. Men have been lost in battle or from the perils of life at sea. Women have died from childbirth or the demands of just living. With this awareness, new mates are found and bonding happens. The despair is quieted.

I walk among the groups. I am open, feeling each and every emotion until exhaustion forces me to sit.

Daylight begins to fade. There is a cool breeze from the ocean. Returning to the altar, my jacket is still rolled up as a pillow on the tabletop. I shake it out. One sleeve needs to be untangled and I slip it on. It's warm. Feels good. I look up. There is no more music and no more people.

The mile-and-a-half walk to my hotel in town takes time. Passing by each boulder, I think I can hear them trying to say something to me. I wonder what else these stones have to reveal. What other stories are to be told. Nearing town, a gentle "moooo" greets me. The cow rubs her neck on a rough megalith. Maybe tomorrow when I'm not so tired, the standing stones will tell me more.

Ж

THE ANGEL WITH A BROKEN WING

"Daddy, Daddy, DADDY!" cries my three-year-old daughter.

Looking through the bars of the gate I had just closed behind me, I see her grief-stricken face. One hand clutches the metal design of the gate, her left hand and arm pushing out, grasping, trying to touch me. Trying to hold me back, trying to prevent me from leaving. I have left before, to work, to attend classes, etc., but she knows this time is different.

I turn back, and she rushes to me through the open gate, throws her arms around my leg, in a futile attempt to stop my departure. Holding her in my arms on my lap as I sit on the top step, I try to say the right words. Some of the words come out as squeaks as my body experiences its own grief. But what are words uttered at a time of total despair? Holding her tight and rocking a little, I try to give reassurance that I will return.

Her mother comes out to the deck, her own face glistening from tears. Experiencing yet again the breakup of a marriage. She picks up our daughter and retreats to the house without looking at me. It is difficult for me to walk to my pickup. My knees are weak, I feel like throwing up. The tears are struggling so hard to be let out, that the pressure has given me a migraine. I start the truck and begin the turn to leave. Looking up, I see my daughter reaching out through the deck railing. Is she waving goodbye or is she still trying to touch me, to hold me, to keep me from leaving? My hands are busy turning the steering wheel. I can't respond. I look away.

It is hard to see the driveway, my eyes are so full of tears. Fortunately, the car tracks are worn so deep, the truck almost steers itself. At the bottom, I pull over and stop before I drive out onto the busy highway.

By the time my daughter was about five years old, our visits had evolved into a pattern. Twice weekly visits, eating supper, then returning her home. Sometimes, she came home with me for an overnight. The evening meal was very important, she was hungry for meat. Her diet at home consisted mainly of root vegetables. This concerned me. I often sent her home with a "care" package of ground beef and fresh fruit, which she picked out.

Even though we had a predictable routine, it never seemed to be enough...for either of us. I could tell she was hurting. Often, she would sit on the seat next to me, pull up and hug her knees, rocking back and forth. She was unable to put into words her pain.

My lap continued to be a place of refuge, a sanctuary for my daughter. My truck had a bench seat, so often after supper she would lie down with her head against me. Sometimes, when still small she would sit on my lap as I drove her home.

Our routine was enlivened with adventures. Her first airplane ride. A forty-five-minute flight including a buzz of her home in west Marin and actually flying through a small cloud. The plane was so small, she sat on my lap so she could see out.

A glider flight (new for me, too) above the hills in the South Bay. Again, she sat on my lap, as we both felt the butterflies in our stomachs. The plane was very quiet, gliding along the very top of the coastal hills, then swooping down into a valley. The pilot pulled back on the stick and the plane responded, catching a thermal and shooting up the face of the hills we had just glided down. This adventure was over too soon for both of us.

A helicopter shuttle ride took us to San Francisco International Airport. The ride was also a first for me. We flew to Denver, then on a small midwestern airline to Dodge City. Spent a wonderful week on the farm, both of us wrapped in family love. My uncle, a Flying Farmer, crowded the three of us into the tiny cockpit of his small airplane. My lap, once again, became the familiar place for my daughter to sit. Together, we drove a huge diesel tractor. She couldn't reach the pedals but enjoyed steering the monster machine from her perch on my lap.

Up in the air again, we rode a hot air balloon above the Napa Valley early in the morning. Interesting, but we both agreed that once was enough. The adventure of flying up in the sky gave my daughter a broader perspective of the world around her. In doing this, I hoped she would be set free to soar.

But she still seemed earthbound, unable to open her wings and fly free. One weekend visit, she posed for me while I created a sculpture. I captured the image of a little angel with a broken wing. She could still fly, but with difficulty. I did what I could. I gave her love, and time, and more adventures.

When she was about eight years old, we returned to western Kansas. Spring. The wheat, tall, dense, and very green made the prairie appear as an ocean of undulating waves, blown by the wind. One could almost feel seasick, surrounded by the movement, nudged by gusts. We ventured deep into a field, pressing through stalks taller than my daughter.

We lay down and marveled at how quickly one could get lost. The rich, juicy smell of growing wheat filling our senses.

"Hey, Dad," she asked. "Have you ever left your body and… well, gone somewhere else?"

"Yes," I said, "Many times. Have you? Tell me about it."

"Nah, not now. Let's go."

We left the field and the next day returned to California.

I watched my daughter for signs of "out-of-body" experiences but didn't see any. However, it did appear she was becoming more comfortable in her body and in the world around her. Maybe this was her maturing, or maybe her wings were healing enough to fly on her own. Maybe both.

She joined in the planning of the next adventures, and together we studied National Geographic world maps. At age nine she still had a little girl's fascination with princesses and castles. No better place for castles than the Loire Valley in France. Even though many of my friends advised against it, Easter vacation found us in Paris, preparing to drive down the Valley.

Wearing her beautiful, new Easter dress, she and I joined the crowd of worshipers at Notre Dame Cathedral on a cold, bleak, late winter day. Inside, she stood on a small ledge, her back against a column. Leaning forward against me, she could see above the heads of the worshipers. The service with the music, choir and organ, the incense, and the age-old pageantry filled us with the celebration of spring and new life.

After an hour, we exited through a side door onto the banks of the Seine. The goddess Eastre was showing herself everywhere. The gray sky, now filled with sun, brought warm breezes. Tulips released their tight, light green buds, and colorful flowers opened and expanded in the sun. People ate or napped on blankets spread close together along the riverbank. All that was needed, I thought to myself, were a few pairs of cavorting bunny rabbits. This was Easter, the celebration of rebirth and new life.

Castles, castles, castles, endless castles. Accompanied by our trusty Michelin Guide, we stopped at every castle on our way through the Loire Valley. An overnight stay in the castle/film set for the movie "Beauty and the Beast" was somewhat disappointing (there was no "Beast"). We did sleep in a room with puffy fabric on the walls instead of wallpaper. And topped off the visit with a delicious breakfast of hot chocolate and croissant.

On the third day, our Michelin Guide indicated another castle on a ridge above the highway. I pulled over to study the Guide, looking for a description. My daughter looked out the window and said, "Enough, Dad, I've had enough castles."

Driving on, we decided to have a picnic. A small, roadside store furnished us with sandwiches of bread, butter, ham, and cheese. We added a bottle of mineral water "with gas." A few miles (or kilometers) later we drove up a dirt road to a "a site of antiquity," as our guide indicated. The ruins of an old Roman aqueduct, a few of the ancient arches remaining, were the perfect stop for lunch. We sat on some stone blocks. Looking out across the beautiful valley, we could just make out more of the Roman ruins on the other side.

Halfway through lunch, my daughter jumped up, selected a heavy stone, and said, "We picked up the stones over there and carried them here and started building the arch."

The hairs on my arms stood up. I could feel a shift in the world around me. Looking across the valley, the old aqueduct seemed to be nearly finished. I asked my daughter a few questions about where she was. She didn't seem to hear me. She came over and finished her lunch. Back on the road again, she didn't want to talk about the aqueduct.

Another ancient site indicated by our Michelin Guide and another stop, this time at an old Roman fort. As we explored the ruins, my daughter had no reaction to the rooms or paths. She gave no response to my questions about Roman times.

We were nearing the end of the Loire Valley when we approached a sign, in both French and English, advertising "Riding Horses for Rent." We were met by a happy, motherly woman who could speak English.

"Would you like to see the horses?" She took my daughter's hand and the two walked to the stables, intently talking horses.

"I know about the wild American Mustangs," the woman said. "But are there other wild horses in America?"

My daughter, who loved horses, began a long story about the wild ponies of Chincoteague Island, off the coast of Virginia.

The woman was interested and asked her many questions.

The stable was a large stone and timber structure built in the early 1800s. The horses were beautiful. As the conversation about wild horses came to an end, I asked if we could rent two horses for a ride.

"Oh, no, no," the woman answered. "The horses are still eating, and then they must have their rest. At least for one hour."

We decided to skip the ride and be on our way. I wanted to reach Nantes before dark. In the heart of the city was a huge, dark castle. The main attraction was the fully restored dungeon, with all the torture machines and equipment in place. We lasted about ten minutes, when my daughter said she had had enough. This place caused her stomach to hurt.

Mine also.

We left the next morning to return to Paris for one more day. I was saving the best for last (or so I thought). One more castle, actually an old Roman fort ruin, now a museum. Deep within there was a room with only one exhibit, the Unicorn in Captivity. This artwork had been a favorite of my daughter. She had a large poster of it hanging in her room. I thought she would be excited by seeing the original. Naw…her poster had better and brighter color.

Returning up through the fort/museum hallways, we emerged into a large room. My daughter stopped and stared.

"That was a cold bathtub, and over there was the hot one. Along the wall, on this side were dressing rooms."

The hair on my arms stood on end. To my eyes, it was just a large, empty room. We turned and started up the wide staircase. A leather suit of Roman armor was mounted on a stand. We stopped. She began exploring the different layers of leather, touching each one.

"Under all these layers," she said, "we wore a wool wrap, kinda like a diaper. But it's not here."

We turned and continued up the stairs. At the next landing were more displays of Roman attire. She had no reaction or interest.

My daughter did not want to, or was even able to talk about, a possible past life bleeding through. I never observed this again. However, years later when she was about eighteen, living in Italy, she related an experience to me. One night, while visiting an old hilltop town, she was sitting on the top of an ancient wall, the valley spread out below. The fog moved in. Through the darkness, she heard the sounds of men marching along the base of the wall. She could make out the *clink, clink, clink* of armor and the thumping of men's feet.

"Maybe," she said, "I did live in Italy, in Roman times."

Again, she didn't want to explore the possibility. But today, thirty-five years later, she is living in Italy with her Italian husband and two kids who are growing up Italian.

Meanwhile, as she grew older, more travels, more flights. Cayman Island in the Caribbean, with its white sand beaches and hours of snorkeling through the colorful coral. Maui, with its black sand beaches. Alaska. A seaplane ride to meet a small, overnight boat to a majestic glacier. The boat rocking gently in the night as the huge wall of ice "calved" huge frozen blocks from the face. Going ashore, to wander around the blocks of ice with their brilliant blue deep cracks. The sandy soil slowly being pushed up in front, building a fresh mound below the towering wall of ice.

When my daughter was thirteen, her mother had a stroke.

"You can come live with me," I said. A week later, she did. I moved off my live-aboard sailboat to a small apartment. When school started the next fall, we moved to a house close enough for her to ride her bike to high school.

A year later, my daughter came to me.

"I want to do something," she said. "All the kids are doing drugs or doing sex. I want to DO something."

"What would you like to do?" I asked. "Think about it and let me know."

A week later, she did.

"I want to go to Russia," she said. "Maybe I can help with the thaw that Gorbachev's talking about. I found a tour for high school kids, a week in Moscow and a week in St. Petersburg. Only costs Five thousand dollars."

"Five thousand! A new Toyota pickup is only two thousand," I said. "Someone could live in Italy for a year for that."

"Oh, yeah?" she said. "Sounds good to me!"

So began a year of preparation, for doing something.

Negotiating with her school to take junior year abroad.
Italian visa.
Finding a family to stay with in Florence.

Updating passport.

Looking for school in Florence.

No exchange school, enroll in a language/art school.

All this and more she accomplished on her own, standing on her own two feet, stretching and flapping her wings. Preparing to take off on her own.

A ride to the airport, a goodbye hug, and I watched as my daughter walked to the boarding gate to fly to Italy. She stepped out of line, turned, reached out her hand and said,

"Bye Dad. See ya."

Her wing was healed.

HEART OF LIGHTNESS I

"Me... me... me...."

Welton can hear the calling, or does he feel it? Or is he sensing the very loud beating of his own heart in the early morning stillness? No, he knows it's the stone talking to him.

As agreed, Welton has arrived at the quarry gate, in the foothills of the Sierras, at 6:30 am.

The early crew who service the quarry equipment open the gate. They wave a greeting. Welton follows them in, up the dirt road to the flat area with the machine shop, various other buildings, and the gigantic wire saw used for cutting granite boulders dug out of the mountain side.

"There's a big truck coming in today," one of the crew says as Welton pulls into the turnaround. "Park over there out of the way so the driver can jockey his rig into the loading area."

"Me... me... me...." Welton can still hear the call.

Welton parks, stops at the machine shop, grabs a white hard hat with the word "VISITOR" painted on it, and eagerly begins looking for the stone calling out to him. This is Welton's fourth visit to the quarry to find the right stones for his sculptures. He knows the routine and licks his lips with anticipation. Each trip to the quarry has been a unique experience. This time the stone is for a large commission...a hoped-for commission.

All is dark gray, almost black, even in the bright morning sun. Everywhere it is the same very dark gray, the ground under foot, the boulders, the broken slabs, and the buildings. No plants, even weeds, grow here. There is no color. Even the huge machine used to move the granite blocks is coated with black dust.

Welton knows that somewhere in this heart of dark grayness is the right stone. He believes it, he hears it, he feels it. Now begins the fun of finding it. He scrambles over and around piles of granite offcuts from the wire saw. In his pocket he carries a spray can of DayGlo bright green paint and a 24-ounce hammer. As per his agreement with the yard boss, Welton has until 8:00 am at which time he must be in the meeting room so that everyone knows where he is. Until then, the quarry crew is aware there's a "VISITOR" running around somewhere on the job site.

"Me... me... me...." The call continues.

The collection of stones covers about a square city block in area. When the pile gets too big, a bulldozer is brought in to push the scrap cutoffs over the side of the mountain, down into the valley and the small lake below. Welton has been tempted, but never explored the stones over the side of the hill. The pile is too dangerous, too unstable. Also, the violent tumble could cause cracks unseen to the eye.

Welton is looking for a specific shape of granite, an end cut.

A month ago, he submitted a sculpture proposal to the architectural committee of a new hospital being built in Washington, DC. Even though there has been no response, Welton is determined to proceed with his creation. He likes the design, he's energized by it, and that's enough motivation to find the right stone and start to carve.

The giant blocks of granite, many the size of a Volkswagen van or larger, weighing 50 tons or more, quarried from the side of the mountain, are taken to the wire saw where one end is sawn off to create a flat surface. Gauging from this flat surface, the next useable slabs or blocks can be sawn. The first saw cut creates an end cut much like the heel on a loaf of bread. It is sawn flat on one side; the other side retains the natural rough texture of the boulder. Welton can see the sculpture design requiring this shape in his mind.

"Me... me... Me!" The call is getting louder.

Welton sits down on a block, takes a few deep breaths. Images of the sculpture float across the screen of his mind. He can see, or maybe sense, the creation from all sides, and sometimes from inside the stone itself. Occasionally, he sees the sculpture placed in the center of the busy lobby. It's the focus of five or six corridors radiating out into the hospital.

In the vast field of stones, there are many possible candidates, but each is either too large or too small. However, a small cutoff catches his eye. It's almost a perfect oval, seven feet long and three-and-a-half-feet wide. About eleven inches tall in the middle, it would make a perfect landscape stone. Placed on the surface of a yard, it would look like the very top of a huge boulder poking out from just under the ground.

Welton taps on the stone with his hammer, listening for possible cracks. "Tick, tick, tick," comes the sound from the hammer blows. It's good. If the sound had been "thock, thock, thock," that would indicate a crack in the stone, perhaps invisible to the eye. Smiling, Welton shakes up the can of DayGlo Green, spray paints a ten-inch stone, and sets it on the newfound granite.

Suddenly, there is color in the huge collection of dark grayness. This little, bright green dab of color can be seen from any place in the scrap yard, even from the quarry buildings.

"Me! Me! Me!" The call is urgent.

Continuing his search through piles of scrap, the beckoning comes to Welton even louder. He knows his stone is—

"There you are!" shouts Welton. "I knew it. I knew it!"

Dancing around the stone, he tests for cracks in a number of places. "Tick, tick, tick, tick." All good. The stone is about six-feet wide and fifteen-feet long, too long for his trailer. But Welton knows he can cut the length down to fit. After placing another bright green signal stone on top of the prize, Welton checks his watch, 7:50 am, just enough time to make it back to the lunch-room by 8:00 am.

He turns to leave, stops, kneels down on the edge of the stone, and places his hand on the rough surface.

"Thanks," he says, "for calling to me."

The quarry crew is just filing into the meeting room. Welton joins them and sits to the side. He recognizes a few from his previous visits and gives a nod. Larry, the yard boss, stands.

"Good morning, guys," he says. "Same ol', same ol', today. Blasting at eleven o'clock, transport arriving this afternoon. And Welton's here to pick out the perfect stone—from our scraps—for his sculpture."

A little chuckle arises from the crew.

"Hi, guys," says Welton. "Don't worry about me, I'll stay out of your way. I'll be out in the cutoff pile—I mean the scrap pile."

Another chuckle.

"Let me know when you've found your stone," says Larry.

"I've already got two," says Welton. "One is pretty big."

"Oh, good," says Larry. "Paul, before you go up, have Welton show you his stones. Drop them off in the number two bay. The load for transport is in number one."

With the scraping of chairs and the thumping of heavy work boots, the crew leave to their various quarry jobs.

Welton asks Paul about his family as they walk to the machine shop.

"I got a son now," exclaims Paul. "My wife was expecting the last time you were here. Everyone is doing fine."

"Yeah, I remember. She was having some difficulties. Glad she's okay."

Paul stops, turns to Welton, clears his throat, and says, "You got a kid, maybe you can understand. I was pretty worried. Didn't realize it until it was all finished and she was fine."

"I understand," says Welton, smiling. "Been there, done that."

The men walk on, side by side, an unspoken bonding. They turn the corner into the shop. There before them is the giant forklift. The men are dwarfed by its size. The massive wheels rising in front of them are over eight feet tall with three-feet-wide treads. The huge forks, resting now on the ground, can lift a block of granite larger than a camper van, weighing over fifty tons.

Paul starts to climb the steel ladder to the driver's control station above the tires. He pauses, turns to Welton. "Maybe you can understand. I'm not sure I do. I've stopped riding my motor-cycle so much. I guess working around all the dangers here at the quarry is enough. I mean, I've got a kid now."

"Yep, I did the same," replies Welton. "Never rode again, once the kid came."

The machine starts with a mighty roar and Paul drives it out into the morning light.

"I can see two green markers," Paul hollers down.

"That's it," says Welton. He gives the thumbs up.

Paul brings the larger stone to the loading bay and lays it down on some smaller blocks. This way he can slide the forks out from under the stone more easily. Later, nylon lifting straps can be slipped in and placed under the stone for loading onto Welton's trailer.

While Paul returns to pick up the smaller stone, Welton sets up his gas-powered stone saw. It looks like a heavy-duty chain saw, but with a circular blade, not a chain. The large, twelve-inch blade has industrial diamond teeth, fabricated to cut granite. Paul returns, drops off the second stone, and helps Welton set up a water hose for cooling the saw blade.

Larry drives up in his pickup. "Hey, Welton! Get in. We're about to blast at the quarry face. Gotta clear this whole area."

Paul maneuvers the forklift to a protected area behind the walls of the shop.

Larry drives down almost to the front gate. "Sometimes, rarely, large chunks of granite fly off the blast site."

"Whoooomp! Boom!" The sound of the blast echoes across the valley.

Back at the loading area, Welton envisions the height of the sculpture and what it will look like, measures the length of his trailer, and begins the cut. Welton smiles, remembering when he learned to execute the first initial cut on a sculpture, squaring off the base. This allows the stone to be stood up, making the design more apparent in the vertical position.

The quarry crew begins to come in for lunch. They watch as Welton saws, back and forth from side to side across the width of the stone, making the cut deeper with each pass. The three-and-a-half-inch deep cut is finished. The men are curious, never having seen such a small machine sawing granite.

Welton sets the saw down and places twelve steel wedges in the saw cut. Striking with a small sledgehammer, Welton drives the steel wedges down into the groove. As they're driven tighter, the wedges ring with a high-pitched response. He selectively strikes different wedges to make all wedges ring at the same tone. This means they're all the same tightness, exerting the same splitting force on the stone. If they aren't uniform, the cut might split unevenly.

Realizing that he has pounded as hard as he can, Welton asks if anyone has an eight-pound sledge. One of the crew brings over a hammer. He continues striking the wedges with more powerful blows. Welton stops, holds his finger to his lips to hush the crowd. A faint, very high-pitched scream comes from the stone. He pauses, listening. The granite is tearing itself apart, crystal by crystal. When the scream softens, Welton picks up the smaller hammer, and with a mighty blow, strikes one of the middle wedges.

POW! Splash!

The lower part of the fifteen-foot stone breaks off and drops into the mud.

"Whoa, that's great!" The guys are impressed.

The break is even. Welton lets out a breath. He had split stones before, but never one this large.

The squared-off stone will be easy to stand upright...the beginning of a sculpture.

Welton picks up and counts his wedges. It's easy to lose them in the mud. He joins the crew in the lunchroom and answers their many questions about how he carves the granite and what tools he uses. There's a good feeling of camaraderie between men who work stone.

After lunch, Paul helps Welton load his pickup and trailer, using nylon lifting straps and the overhead travel crane. Granite weighs approximately two hundred pounds per cubic foot. Thus, a stone's weight can be determined by measuring the volume. Even though calculating an odd shape is a challenge, Welton estimates the large stone at about forty-five hundred pounds and the smaller one at fifteen hundred pounds. The truck, a three-quarter ton flatbed pick up, can carry almost three thousand pounds, so the smaller stone will be an easy load for the truck bed. The trailer, with its dual axels, has a load rating of six thousand pounds, no problem for the larger stone.

Larry comes over to check on the load. At fifteen cents per pound, the six thousand pounds of material will cost nine hundred dollars. Larry pauses, probably calculating in his head. "How about five hundred?" he says.

"Okay," says Welton, feeling relieved. It's a risk to purchase materials before obtaining a sculpture contact. But he wants to be fair. "I did come up with a little more."

Larry laughs. "Don't worry about it. I have to put something down in my order book. I'm really charging you for Paul's time and the machine. You picked a couple of easy stones, didn't take much time."

"Well, thanks ..."

"I enjoy doing business with you," says Larry, "The crew really seem to get a lift from your visit. Guess it gives them a break from the daily—oh, don't forget to tie down your load."

"Got my ratchet straps and chain tightener right here."

Larry turns to leave, stops, and says with a shrug, "You might as well take the cut off with you. That way Paul won't have to take it back to the scrap pile."

One more stone is added to the trailer's load, as there isn't room on the truck. This will be close to maximum capacity. Welton looks under the trailer. There's still a margin left on the overload springs. Welton calculates the extra stone to weigh approximately twelve hundred pounds.

This scrap stone will sit in Welton's studio yard for sixteen years, until it's the perfect stone for his final sculpture.

Welton starts the truck and pulls out. He's not overloaded but is very heavy. He checks his brakes before starting down the mountain. Halfway down, he sees a large semi coming up. The road isn't designed for two-way traffic. Welton pulls over as far as possible, avoiding the deep drainage ditch. His front tire starts to slip, or was that just a bump? Welton stops. He hopes he's allowed enough room for the large truck to continue up the road without slowing down.

Sitting, waiting at the side of the road, Welton tries to relax, but his mind starts to chatter. He's excited about finding the perfect stone for the hospital sculpture. But his trailer is wider than his pickup. *Is there enough room for the semi to pass?*

Can the banks of the ditch hold the weight of my truck and trailer? Or will they cave in?

Can I make it back to my studio before dark? Because, you know...

What's the response from the DC hospital?

Have they even responded?

The ground shakes as the semi drives past without slowing, with mere inches separating the two vehicles.

Whew, one less thing to worry about.

Welton continues down the mountain and settles into the five-hour drive to his sculpture studio in the Bay Area. The only route to the freeway from the quarry is through Fresno on city streets. It's slow going with frequent stop-and-go traffic. Welton checks his rearview mirror and sees the trailer wheels smoking. The surge brakes can't distinguish between just a slowdown and a full-on stop. They've become the slowing down and the full stop brakes for both the truck and the heavy trailer.

Welton pulls into a restaurant parking lot. Getting out of the cab, he can smell the burning, acrid odor of hot brake pads. They need time to cool. Sitting in a booth inside, Welton orders a burrito and Mexican coffee.

Back on the road, Welton merges with Highway 99, slipping into heavy truck traffic. A few miles north, Welton crosses over to Interstate 580. Driving is much easier. He picks up speed. Welton hears a pop, then feels a pull to the left. In the rearview mirror, Welton sees patches of black rubber being thrown from a tire. He slowly pulls onto a wide, grassy shoulder. Only shreds of the tire remain. Welton's thankful for the trailer's dual axels. If not for them, the trailer would have turned over, spilling tons of stone and hurting who knows how many people. The trailer's forward tire has saved him.

Welton doesn't have a spare. The trailer requires a special tire. Using a one-ton hydraulic jack, Welton is barely able to lift one side to remove the damaged tire and rim. He lowers the trailer and removes the jack to prevent anyone from stealing his rig. There's nothing he can do to secure his load of granite.

There's a tire shop in the next town. They have to order the special trailer tire, which can be delivered the next day. Welton orders two and heads home.

The next morning, Welton drives three hours back to the tire shop to pick up the repaired wheel. Returning to the trailer, he jacks up the load and replaces the wheel. On the way back down, the shop also replaces the tire on the other side.

With the two new tires and his full load, Welton returns to his studio-workshop. It's dark when he arrives. The last two days have been hard work. He checks his mailbox, hoping for a positive response from the hospital in DC.

HEART OF LIGHTNESS II

Today is the day! Welton is going to set up the new granite stone. It has been three days, three very long days since he returned with his load from the quarry. The dog's been sick, there was a doctor's appointment he'd forgotten, and, and … but now he's focused on the job of setting up the stone and beginning the sculpture. With his forklift, Welton offloads the truck first. The eye-catching landscaping stone is set in the front of his stone pile, with the hopes someone will purchase it.

The "free" scrap off-cut is delegated to the back of the pile, over the weeds, and set on two 4X4 wooden blocks.

There it will sit for sixteen years, out of sight and out of mind. Over time, other stones will be brought in from the quarry, and crafted at the studio into sculptures, then left for their new homes. The scrap offcut just sits there, until it will be the perfect stone for Welton's last sculpture.

Welton is working alone. He has a young man who comes in to help a few afternoons a week in exchange for the opportunity to learn stone sculpting. Welton cannot afford to hire an assistant. Today is not a day with help, and he is just fine with that. His mind is filled with the sculpture images. Images which are demanding to be created in stone.

Using the forklift, Welton removes the new stone from the trailer. He smiles as he remembers the huge forklift at the quarry which could lift and move fifty tons. The capacity of his machine is three tons. With two nylon straps, one on each side, the stone is hoisted to the vertical standing position and placed on the level concrete working pad, with wedges underneath to adjust the plumb. The smooth, sawn side of the granite faces the sun.

It is magnificent! Welton feels its presence. His heart gives a little flutter, and a grin spreads across his face.

The images for the sculpture, which have been crowding his mind for weeks, are impatient to start. But first, the surface must be washed free of the quarry mud. The pressure water washer removes the sticky, black mud and also forces water into any tiny cracks. The sun quickly dries the nonporous surface. Any small cracks would continue to weep, revealing their existence. The monolith is flawless.

The challenge is now transforming the ethereal world of mental images to the hard, physical reality of a creative design in stone. Welton does not draw or even sketch his ideas. He has found it too frustrating to attempt the rendering of a three-dimensional idea within the confines of two dimensions on a sheet of paper. Sometimes Welton, confiding within himself, toys with the possibility that he is dealing with a fourth or even a fifth dimension when he explores potential sculptural images in his mind. He has never been able to explain how he can see the sculpture from all sides simultaneously, even from inside the stone. As far as he knows, no sculptor has ever addressed this ability to see.

Welton is very comfortable being alone, with no one to distract him from the creative process. He uses colored sidewalk chalk to indicate where the first cut is to be made. Different colors indicate surfaces deep within the stone. Sometimes when beginning a sculpture, he just picks up a stone saw and starts to carve, trusting to his creative muse to guide his hands. But today, he feels the need to expand the image within the overall huge stone. His design seems, at first, to be too small. If it is enlarged, he is concerned that too much stone will be removed and thus weaken the finished sculpture. Welton wants the sculpture to be as open as possible, to have a playful contrast between the solidness of granite and the view through the stone to the other side.

As Welton ponders where to inscribe the chalk marks, much to his surprise, the images in his mind become even more vivid. He juggles the relationship between the solid stone and where to create the opening. In his mind, the internal surfaces of the design have evolved and are now glowing with a vivid, bright light. The title of the sculpture flashes into his consciousness: *HEART OF LIGHTNESS.*

The sculpture has a name, a title. The stone is no longer "the stone," it comes alive, it is the *Heart of Lightness.* Days before at the quarry, the stone had called out, "Me, me, me!" Now, with its identity, the sculpture speaks to him not so much in words, but as a valid part of Welton's psyche. It is as if there are three entities co-creating to produce the sculpture. Maybe all three, in a broad sense, are Welton himself. In the physical world is Welton with the tools of his craft in hand. In the non-physical world is the creative muse and her images. The stone sculpture is a combination of both the physical—very hard granite—and its ability to communicate from a non-physical world.

There are goosebumps on Welton's arms. His heart feels as if it is about to explode, in a good way. Or is it a God way? This is pure joy, joy which passes all understanding. Welton basks in the sunlight, feeling its warmth and the excitement of co-creation.

Chalk lines are quickly laid out, guidelines for the saw cuts. In the past, Welton has created large oval shapes for the openings in his sculpture. As this design is sketched, Welton sees a new shape emerging, deep within the stone. He uses a different color chalk for this new, inner shape. The cold granite, now warming in the sun, seems to know what it wants, what it likes.

"Thanks," says Welton, "for talking to me."

Keeping his left hand near the chalk lines on the stone, Welton can feel the conversation taking place between the three of them.

"What's the inner design, the inner shape doing protruding into the opening space?"

Immediately, Welton sees the inner shape, the new, deeper surface reflecting a bright, white glow from within the sculpture. He understands. Dark granite can be made to look almost white by using a finishing technique of pulverizing the surface, breaking up the crystal makeup.

Welton considers adding a light source to this sculpture. Over the last few years, he has added the element of flowing water to his creations, but interest in "water features" is diminishing. One of his creations in New York City has been shut down due to a city-wide ban on water sculptures. His proposal to the DC hospital offered an either/or design. It's time to decide, before the first cuts are made. In the heart of the sculpture is light.

Using a small saw, he outlines the design, starting at the bottom so the saw's cooling water will not wash away the chalk. With a larger saw, Welton makes the first cuts. It is vital to open the stone as soon as possible. If there are any internal flaws or cracks, it is better to make their existence known. Welton uses his large, diamond-toothed chain saw, powered by an external hydraulic power source. It's heavy and powerful, but can make a plunge cut through the ten to twelve inches of granite.

Welton makes three parallel cuts, three-fourths of an inch apart, about fourteen inches long. Using a hammer and tapered chisel, he breaks out the two exposed segments.

Light! There is daylight shining through the solid granite. The window is only about two inches wide and maybe thirteen inches long, but the stone has been opened. From this reference view-point, the sculpture can be created. He will be able to work from both sides, seeing how deep the cuts into the mass of granite can be made.

Welton begins making a series of parallel saw cuts and chisels out the stone between the cuts. If this segment is too wide, it's difficult to remove. Too narrow, it's a waste of cutting time. Once the rough shape has been established, he turns a small saw blade to cut sideways, shaving the remaining stone to create the desired shape.

Many of Welton's early granite sculptures were water features. He once taught a class titled, "A Fountain Is More Than a Rock with a Hole In It." He developed ways to create the pleasing babbling sounds of falling water. If an energetic sculpture was in order, he installed various shaped nozzles to shoot or spray water up in the air. To create a feeling of calm, the surface of the water on the top of the sculpture was smooth and placid. The water would continue its flow over the top edge and down the sides in a thin laminar surface, shimmering in the sunlight or from carefully placed underwater lights.

Later, Welton began adding side-emitting fiber optic lighting to his designs. The flexible plastic cable gave a pleasant, soft light. However, the intensity of light was limited, and the electric light source at the bottom end of the cable required a very noisy cooling fan.

The DC hospital sculpture would stand on a large base which could house the light source. If the hospital architects wanted a water feature, the base could be a basin. Welton was wary of using water. Inexpensive, Chinese "rock with a hole in them" sculptures were flooding the market. His gallery was having difficulty selling unique, one of a kind, site-specific water sculptures. Then, a New York City ban on excessive water use resulted in his sculptures being turned off for a few months.

The Heart of Lightness is a perfect candidate for fiber optic lighting. A channel, deep enough and wide enough to hide the optic cable is cut into one side of the opening. The light will shine across to illuminate the other side of the opening, but will be buried deep enough in the slot to be hidden from the eyes of a viewer.

Welton wonders when, or if, the hospital will reply to the proposed sculpture design. But now that he has begun, he won't stop. The muse has him in her grasp. The sawing and grinding continue day after day. Welton is totally engrossed in his creation. Time stands still. Only the fading of daylight marks the passing of each day. The final design is being revealed. How the light will reflect on the granite surface determines the subtle angles Welton carves in the stone. He feels an urgency to integrate the lighting into the evolving sculpture.

Welton places a short length of optic cable in the carved channel. He returns at night to see what effect the lighting makes on the design. There is not enough illumination.

A new product has reached the market, called LED. It comes in two forms, tiny Christmas lights and in rigid strips for attaching under overhead kitchen cabinets. Welton knows that neither product is the solution. He finds a company in Hong Kong that manufactures LEDs. He phones them direct.

"Do you make a flexible, waterproof LED?" asks Welton.

"Yes," answers the voice on the phone. "We have ten-foot rolls, 35 watts of Light Emitting Diodes, at 12 volts."

"That's a lot of wattage. So much light!"

"The diodes are close together."

"How soon can you send me a ten-foot roll?" asks Welton.

There is a long pause. Finally, the voice says, "We have developed the item. We are just beginning production. We can ship in about two weeks."

Welton finishes carving the design. The areas that will reflect the light are finished by pulverizing the granite surfaces to break up the reflected light. This process makes the stone appear to glow from within.

The LEDs are perfect, lighting the sculpture with a strong, cool white light. Illuminating *Heart of Lightness* is one of the first uses of this new technology.

Welton is pleased. He has combined the age-old sculpting material, granite, with the latest tech product, LEDs.

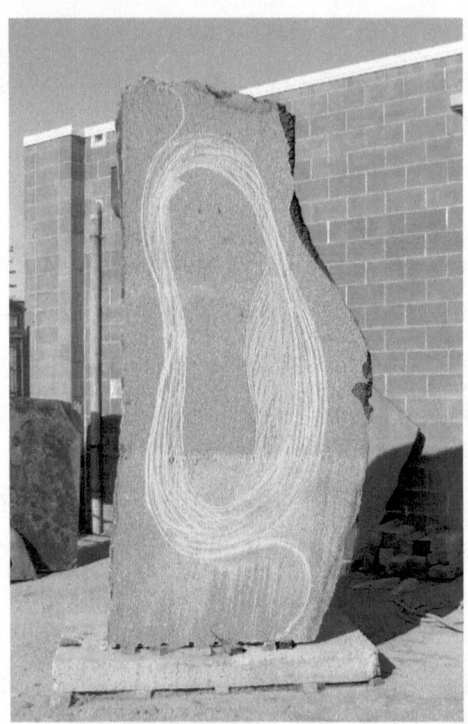

Heart of Lightness
Marked in chalk
First cuts
With the sculptor
Lit at night

HEART OF LIGHTNESS III

It's a challenge getting used to coming home in an elevator. But with his progressive numbness, first the feet, and then the legs, moving from a beautiful Edwardian home with three floors to an apartment was necessary. The new home, all one level, is on the sixteenth floor. The breathtaking view is a plus. But to Welton, it feels like a hotel room. Is this really home?

Welton suggests to the board of directors of the apartment complex that he gift a site-specific sculpture to the building. His offer prompts some strong discussion.

"If we accept this gift," say a few board members, "What's to keep others from wanting their work to be included and installed here?"

"Well," say other members, "just how many professional artists live here in the complex? Let's see what Welton has to offer."

The director turns to Welton. "Why do you want to give us one of your creations?"

"Because this is now my home, and I like living with my work, and there's no room in my tiny apartment for a large, outdoor granite sculpture."

Welton's disability has affected more of his body. He now uses a four-wheeled walker. Its seat provides a comfortable way for him to sit and study the front landscape, both in daylight and at night. The front of the apartment building stretches along a whole city block. The curved entrance drive and lobby fill the center third. The driveway surrounds intense landscaping, the perfect location for the sculpture. It must be large enough not to get lost in the plantings, but not so tall it blocks the view out to the street from the lobby.

This sculpture is special for Welton. He has not created a major work for the last two or three years since his hands became paralyzed and would no longer hold a tool. Welton now depends on Steve, his assistant of fourteen years, to do the physical work of stone carving. He has been a quick learner.

Welton has a feeling that this sculpture will be his last work. It's not an easy feeling. Questions of life and death crowd into his daily thoughts. What's left for him in this life without being able to create with his hands? What about his identity as a sculptor? It has been more than fifty-five years of sculpting. One more piece.

He and Steve search around the pile of accumulated granite blocks at his studio. It would be a long roundtrip to the quarry to select a new stone, and once there, could Welton maneuver his walker through the scrap pile?

They find the cutoff from the *Heart of Lightness* under a pile of weeds. It's outside the pile of unused granite, behind a small tree that has sprung up. The stone was set in this hiding place sixteen years ago. It is wide, but not too tall. Welton knows it's the perfect stone. The rough side could face the street, and the smooth side could be polished, reflecting the lights from the lobby.

Steve, driving the forklift, pulls out the stone and sets it on new blocks. The original blocks have disintegrated over time. A power wash cleans away years of accumulated grime. Welton, in his excitement, can picture the finished stone sitting in the planter box surrounded with lush plants. He can see the stone with a large opening allowing a view of the street from the lobby.

Welton loves the comfortable shape of an oval. He cuts out two oval cardboard patterns using the same formula for each. However, one oval is larger than the other. He places the larger oval on the smooth surface, the side facing the inside lobby. The oval is laying down, the longer dimension almost horizontal. Welton places the smaller oval up and to the right, on the outer, rough side.

When the stone is opened, and the two holes are connected, it will appear that both ovals are the same size, just far apart up a long tunnel, maybe four feet in length. The thickness of the stone at the ovals is actually only about eight inches. This is compressed perspective. The outer opening, being higher up, will allow morning sunlight to shine down through the stone, bringing light into the garden.

Steve saws and carves his way through the granite, connecting the two ovals. It is tedious work for him, because the two openings are not directly opposite each other. Welton sits on his walker watching, trying to contain his frustration. He knows that he could cut through much faster, because he can visualize the design inside the stone. Steve is doing the best he can, and he's very careful. Welton comforts himself, knowing that this is his design, his creation, and that he needs Steve to make it happen.

Over the years of creating sculpture, Welton has become comfortable with his designs changing for the better. He trusts his muse, his creative self. Proportions change, surface finishes morph from intended rough to high polish, and sometimes he adds lighting. The idea of placing the street side oval up and to the right, instead of straight through, is an example of this change. The new idea is more difficult to sculpt, but the resulting offset is beautiful, allowing sunlight to flow through the sculpture, through the heart of lightness.

Welton decides to have Steve carve subtle undulations on the flat face of the sculpture, then polish the surface to a high, reflective shine. The surface will appear to be flat. But, as a person walks past the sculpture, the numerous overhead lights will reflect in the polished face and dance about. The observer's mind will interpret this as movement. It will seem as if the sculpture is moving.

Steve and Welton install the new sculpture in the garden at the front of the complex. They use a hydraulic crane that Welton designed to hoist, swing out, and place the stone at its new home. The landscape committee is energized to redo the plantings to accent the new gift. They even replace the sixty-year-old soil in the planter boxes. Welton installs 24/7 LED landscape lighting for the sculpture. He is pleased.

A small party is organized to welcome the new gift. Welton explains compressed perspective and the appearance of movement by the light reflecting on the surface.

"What is the name of the sculpture?" asks a resident.

"*HOME*" replies Welton, without missing a beat.

THE GIFT OF BALUT

"What am I supposed to do with this?" I ask.

"Eat it," Julita answers.

"In front of all these people?" I ask. "I'm the only one eating. That's impolite."

"No, they'll all experience joy as they watch," she says. "The group will vicariously feel your emotion."

That's quite a responsibly for me, I think.

I'm sitting at a small table in a cramped room with eight or ten people standing very close. The only light comes from an old florescent tube humming on the ceiling. An elderly woman, no taller than I am when seated, steps up to the table. She carries a walking stick in one hand and something wrapped in a cloth in the other. She presents the gift to me.

I ask Julita my question about eating. She continues talking to me, translating when the older lady speaks, and explains what is happening.

Julita's mother has come all the way from her small, provincial village to visit her daughter outside Manila. The gift her mother has brought for me is her way of thanking me and my parents for helping complete her child's education.

Julita lives in faculty housing on the University of the Philippines campus, where she is a professor in the School of Nursing.

About ten years ago, just after the war, my college professor parents helped a young woman, Julita, further her education. Julita lived with our family in Manila as a housekeeper while she attended college. My parents extended their support and sponsored her continued education in the States.

The gift from her mother is a *balut*, a fertilized duck egg, hard-boiled twelve or sixteen days after being laid. If it wasn't boiled, a duck chick would hatch at twenty-eight days.

I have never eaten a *balut*. I recall, as a kid living in Manila, hearing street venders calling out *"Baluuuuuuuut,"* as they jogged along, their eggs nestled in two baskets suspended from a bamboo pole across their shoulders. The vendors' customers desired an evening treat and hoped to experience the supposed aphrodisiac quality of the *balut*. I had watched a friend opening and consuming one of these delicacies, first with curiosity, then with repulsion.

The room is hot, muggy hot, hot like only an evening in Manila can be. The space is oppressive, closing in on me. Or is it just the people surrounding me, moving forward to get a better look? I'm having difficulty breathing. Sweat runs down my armpits.

Placing the egg in my left hand, small end up, I carefully break a hole about the size of a nickel in the end and sprinkle a pinch of coarse, dirty gray sea salt on the exposed interior. I noisily slurp out the liquid. It's warm. Of course it is! What should I expect? Julita's mother has been carrying this precious gift in her hand during a three-hour ride in an open bus. I feign enjoyment. There is a murmur of happy recognition from the assembled group.

The process continues.

Slowly peeling the eggshell about halfway down exposes the innards. Skin stretched over the shape of internal bones, feathers on the skin, only soft and not fully formed. An eye, only a circular shape at this stage. I'm relieved at the low light level in the room. I don't have to look closely.

There's very little odor, for which I'm grateful. Perhaps it's masked by the multitude of human smells filling the room. Taking the first bite is a challenge. The flesh is soft. The taste is mild, similar to poached chicken breast without seasoning. Eating the bones is no problem, like eating the bones in canned sardines or canned salmon. The yoke is almost gone, its role to furnish nutrition to the developing chick nearly accomplished.

I add more salt.

Taking another bite with my eyes closed, I feel something firm like gristle. It's the beak, not yet fully hard. I'm tempted to spit it out, but where would I put it? It goes down with the rest.

The beak intrigues me. It is the most developed of all the parts. Everything, every part of this little creature is folded, wrapped, rolled, and compressed into a very small, tight shape. An egg shape.

If the duck egg had been allowed to continue developing, it would be ready to hatch in a few days. The beak has the power and instinct to break an escape hole in the hard shell which has been the home, the womb, the protection for the little chick for 28 days.

My consumption of *balut* is finished. The gift has been eaten. The assembled group presses forward with pleasant murmurs and joyful smiles on their faces. Julita is happy, too. This has somehow been a confirmation for her. She stays by my side, introducing her relatives to me and translating when needed. The conversations go something like, "Hello, I'm Julita's brother, sister, aunt, uncle, cousin, nephew, niece. Thank you for helping her. I'm very glad you enjoyed the gift of the *balut*."

The next day I leave to continue my backpacking trek around Asia. Somehow, my visit, culminating with eating the *balut*, has brought closure for Julita. My family's gift to the young woman years earlier has come full circle. In ways I do not understand, she is now freed, unentangled from the shell that had protected her as she developed. It had also somehow restricted her further growth and expansion.

For years after her education was complete, Julita all but stopped communication with my family. We would receive the compulsory Christmas card once a year. She never said, "Thank you" to anyone. Maybe she did not know how to voice thankful recognition for the wonderful gift of education. Maybe her "beak" was not developed enough to break out of the strong, loving, supportive shell we all had created around her.

Standing in the doorway of Julita's humble home, saying goodbye, she throws her arms around my waist and says something into my chest. I struggle to bend over, fighting the forty-pound backpack I'm wearing, so my face is close to hers.

Softly, she says, "Thank you," and gives me a hug.

TRIANGLES

The boat hatch slides open, a head pops out.

"Oh, sorry," says the young woman on the dock. "I didn't know anyone was aboard."

"It's okay."

The head and the body of a sturdy young man emerge, pulling a jacket over his broad shoulders. "Would you like to come aboard? I'm Jim."

"Oh, yes. My name is—"

"Careful! The dock's slippery where the sun hasn't dried the dew yet. Here, take my hand."

"Thanks." She steps aboard.

"I'll turn this cushion over," Jim says, "Should be dry underneath."

"I like the color, kinda red orange with a yellow stripe," she says.

"And, if you look close, there's some dark green," Jim says. "I know a weaver who made the fabric for me."

"It's beautiful, but why? Aren't most boat cushions—"

"Because—" Jim interrupts. "I wanted to match my boat's name."

"*Amber*?" she asks, "Like the gemstone?"

"Oh, great!" Jim says. "You got it."

"Of course," she says. "I'm partial. My name's Amber, well, that's my middle name. So, your boat is also named *Amber*?"

"Uh, ah…" Jim sputters, flustered.

"I noticed your boat from up on shore and walked down the dock to check out the name." She shrugs. "I don't know why… just had a desire to…well, you know." She pushes back the hood on her coat, her red/gold hair flashes in the morning sun.

The tea kettle whistles. "I'm making tea," Jim says. "Would you like some?"

"Yes, please. Do you have green or herbal? I've already had coffee this morning."

"Yes, coming up in a moment."

"Careful, it's hot," says Jim. "I hope you like—"

"Oh, Japanese Ceremonial…"

"Not really. This is from a tea bag, not the whole tea ceremony."

Amber takes a sip. "But this is better. The ceremonial tea is too bitter."

They sit quietly. Amber lifts her cup and blows to cool the next sip. She glances at Jim. He's staring at her. She meets his gaze and returns it with a smile but pulls her padded coat tighter as if for protection. "It feels good here in the sun. How did you come to name your boat *Amber*?"

"I like your coat, especially the diamond stitching for padding."

Amber strokes her coat's sleeve. "Um, thanks."

"My folks wanted a girl," Jim says. "But all they got was me." He grimaces. "They planned to have a daughter; they would have named her Amber. So, dad gave her name to his boat. Why do you ask?"

"Oh, it's just that my middle name is—"

"Really? Oh right, you just said it was your middle name," says Jim. "Why don't you call yourself Amber?"

"You know..." She pauses. "You go to school and they call you by your first name. Then it's Social Security, medical records, etc. Some of my friends call me Amber, and it sounds good to me. But then I think, why not Ruby, or Pearl, or even... I decided, when I found a place to live, I would change all my records and information to Amber. Today seems like a good time to try it out."

"Amber is so beautiful and so special!" Jim says. "The color is so very complex, a challenge to paint. And the stone is, is, well, is beautiful! In the cabin below, there's a piece of amber mounted where anyone walking by can touch it."

Moving to the open hatch, Amber looks down into the cabin.

"I see it," she says. "A Touchstone. Some believe it can give one's life direction. So, do you believe that?"

Jim shrugs. "Well, yes and no."

"It looks cozy down in the cabin," she says, "Do you live here? I smell linseed oil. Do you paint?"

"Aummm, what brings you to Port Townsend?" asks Jim.

Amber laughs. "Long story or short?"

"Either, you decide," Jim says, "I have the time."

"Well," Amber says, thinking for a moment. "I believe one should follow their bliss. The problem is finding your bliss."

"Yeah, that's for sure."

"So, after school, and trying a few jobs, I think I've found what I want to do."

"What's that?" asks Jim.

"Too long to go into," answers Amber. "What I'm doing now is deciding where I want to live."

"So, you've decided on Port Townsend," says Jim.

"Not yet, just looking."

"So, why Port Townsend?"

"My mind is spinning with all the images." Amber takes a breath, trying to collect her thoughts. "I have a strong desire to tell it all, even though I don't really know you."

"It's okay," Jim says. "I'm really interested."

Amber nods. "My grandpa, before he died, told me I should go to the Northwest. That I would like it there. After college, I got a job and got caught up in the rat race."

She pauses to sip her tea. "The only times I felt at peace and happy were when I meditated. Do you meditate?"

"Oh yeah…when I have time."

"So," Amber continues. "I kept hearing this little voice saying to go. Sometimes it sounded like my grandpa, and now here I am. I was so excited I couldn't sleep last night. I got up at first light and walked to this boat harbor, and the sea gulls were laughing with me at my joy, and … maybe I'm saying too much?"

"No, no!" Jim leans forward. "The gulls woke me up, too, they sounded different. I think they were telling me to get up and look out… there was someone out there." Jim looks down at his empty cup. "Your openness encourages me to tell you some things, but…"

Amber stands up. "I'm not too bashful to tell you that I have to use the restroom."

"If you're urgent, you can use the one here on the boat," Jim responds. "If you can wait, we could go up to the Maritime Center."

"You're holding my hand again," Amber says as they step off the boat. "I can make it to the building by myself."

"But I need to unlock the Center," Jim replies dropping her hand. "I sense a lot through touch. Sometimes I think I should have been a sculptor, but instead I paint."

"What else are you learning by touching me? And don't just stand there with that silly grin on your face... tell me!"

Jim continues to gaze at her, then says, "I wish this was our second date, I would be less cautious about what I say." He pauses. "I've got an idea... no, two ideas. I could meet you outside the Center, and that would start our second date."

"Wait, wait, wait!" Amber blurts out. "This is going too fast. Who said we were on date number one? And why do you have a key to the Center?"

"Because I teach a class there, a painting class," answers Jim. "And why not? Don't you feel this is more than a casual meeting?"

"Well, what's your second idea? Or do I have to wait until I come out?"

"Yep, second date... second idea."

"That's better. Oh, nice to see you again," Amber says with an exaggerated wave. "When I agreed to a second date, I forgot to tell you that I was hungry... no breakfast this morning."

"Ha! That's my second idea, to go for breakfast," says Jim, taking her hand, "I know a great place in town."

They walk along, both caught up in their own thoughts.

"See that art gallery across the street?" Amber says, breaking the silence. "If they're open after breakfast, I would like to check it out."

"Are you reading my mind?" exclaims Jim, squeezing her

hand. "I was going to take you there… something I want to show you."

Breakfast is awkward. The restaurant echoing with the happy sounds of morning people. Jim seems preoccupied, Amber is quiet, thinking about the painting she saw earlier in the window. Jim pays the bill, and off they go to the gallery, only a short walk from the restaurant.

"Hi Jim, glad you came by," says the gallery owner, a petite brunette bustling with energy. "I just received a check for your painting of the sailboat and Mount Baker."

"That was your painting?" exclaims Amber, "I saw it this morning and was going to come back and maybe buy it! Well, congratulations! Do you have any more?"

"Oh, you are a friend of Jim's?" asks the owner. "I could give you a discount on another. But before we do business, I have to talk with Jim."

She turns away from Amber.

"Jim…I have some bad news…my husband just got transferred and he has to arrive by next Monday. He'll go on ahead and I'll stay and pack up. The hardest part is the gallery. I don't know what to do. I would hate to have to return all the artwork. Maybe someone would like to buy the gallery as is. But we need staff to keep it going. I just don't know—"

"Talk about coincidence!" Amber breaks in. "I'm looking for a job."

"Oh, could you manage the gallery? Do you have any experience?" asks the owner. "I can't pay much, but I really need some help. I guess Jim can give you a good recommendation."

"Oh, for sure!" Jim grins.

"Can you start work today? What was your name again?"

"Amber. Of course I can."

"About two o'clock?"

"Yes! See you then. Bye."

A few steps after leaving the gallery, Amber stops, turns to Jim and questions him. "So that's why you keep looking at me... you really are a painter. Do you want to paint me?"

"I already have... I mean— Yes, I would."

Amber laughs. "Never know what can happen on a second date!"

"Let's go back to my boat," Jim says. "I want to show you something, a painting."

"Okay," says Amber. "But before we go, I have a strong desire to walk out on the pier. It seems like so much is happening so fast, I need to get some fresh air and quiet my mind. I'm enjoying the ride, but I need to stay centered."

"The pier was rebuilt in 2002," says Jim. "Bronze plaques were embedded in the decking to—"

"Jim! look! There's a plaque with *Annie Too*. My grandpa's boat was named *Annie Too*. Oh Jim, hold me... I'm shaking all over. I can feel that my grandpa is here, he must be a spirit guide. He must be guiding me...all these years to come to the Northwest, then a few weeks ago he said to come to Port Townsend. And now..."

"You're crying."

"Tears of joy. I'm witnessing... no, I'm experiencing a powerful connection. My spirit guide, maybe my grandpa, is right here now. My knees feel weak. I need to sit."

"I can feel it too," says Jim. "Here's a bench, or can you make it back to *Amber*? It's more comfortable. There's something I want to tell you."

"I'm ok, I guess I can make to your boat. But let me sit here for a moment. I need to quiet this feeling, this experience."

"Sit in the cockpit. No, no, the other side," says Jim. "I want the sun at your back."

Amber moves. A part of her mind is still up on the pier, thinking about her grandpa. The sun feels good on her back.

"Oh, is that one of your paintings?" she asks as Jim brings out a canvas from the cabin.

"Hang on! I need to tell you something first." Jim sets the painting down, facing away from Amber. "Do you know the story of Pygmalion and Galatea?"

"Do you mean the story of the sculptor falling in love with his creation, and the sculpture comes to life?" asks Amber.

"Yes, I like the painting done by Jean Leon Gerome," says Jim, "It shows so much love and tenderness as the sculptor embraces the figure."

"It's a nice fantasy," says Amber. "But... "

"Well, I thought I would try to paint a Beautiful Woman with whom I could fall in love and have her materialize," says Jim. "I have tried many paintings of women but none that I could fall in love with."

"Or they with you."

"Right..."

"Did they have as nice a figure, as nice a butt, as Galatea?"

"Ahhh..."

"Maybe it's not love," says Amber. "Maybe lust. Sounds like a male fantasy to me. What do we know, what does Pygmalion know about her personality? She might be a real bitch!"

"No, no, not the woman I would be painting."

"How could you tell?" asks Amber.

Jim falls silent, returns the painting to the cabin without showing Amber the canvas.

Jim returns, just as Amber stands up to leave.

"I'm sorry," says Amber. "I didn't mean to rain on your parade."

"Maybe you're right."

"I could see where this was going...from your viewpoint," she says. "You want to paint me. And then we live happily ever after."

Jim, looking down, says, "Yes, but with all the synchronicity happening...you know, your name, my boat's name..."

"I think you're trying too hard," says Amber.

"But don't you believe in synchronicity?"

"Of course I do. But you can't make it happen. You have to step back and listen to your insides," says Amber. "I think you're practicing 'fake it until you make it', and that's—"

"What's wrong with that?" asks Jim.

"You're sabotaging yourself, instead of learning what you need to learn to improve and succeed. You're pretending."

"But—" says Jim.

"There's nothing wrong with painting beautiful women," says Amber. "Just don't expect love to follow."

"I would still like to paint you," says Jim.

"Maybe," says Amber. "Just don't paint me the color of cold marble, and paint more of me than a beautiful butt." She laughs, steps closer to Jim, and kisses him on the cheek. "I've got to go, I have to get ready for my new job."

About five o'clock, Jim pokes his head into the gallery door. "Are you through with work? Would you like to go to dinner?"

"Uhhhh. Well," says Amber, "I still have to close up, and—"

"I can help with that," replies Jim.

"And I'm pretty tired," says Amber. "I was thinking that I would just grab a sandwich to go, spend some quiet time, and get to bed early. It's been a big day."

"Yeah, that's for sure," Jim agrees. "I don't want to be a pest."

Amber reaches out and touches his arm. "You're not a pest, I just need some 'me' time. I want to think about all that's happened today."

Smiling, Jim says, "Go for it, see you tomorrow."

Amber walks up the street to a deli. Just as she arrives, someone places a "closed" sign in the window. She knocks and the door opens.

"Sorry, we're closed," says a young man.

"Oh, I just want a sandwich to go," says Amber.

"Ok, we can do that," answers the man. "We usually stay open longer, but tonight my sister and I are going to Bible study class."

"Thanks so much," says Amber. "I'm pretty tired and don't want to go to a restaurant."

"Are you new in town?" asks the sister, coming forward. "What sandwich would you like? We haven't put the ham in the fridge yet, it's really good. I would suggest provolone cheese and—"

"Sounds wonderful," says Amber.

"Would you like to join our study group?" asks the young man. "We're always looking for more young people."

"Oh, thanks," says Amber. "I'm really tired. Maybe another time."

As she turns to leave, Amber notices a poster in the window announcing the Port Townsend Wooden Boat Festival in a few weeks.

Her job at the art gallery becomes more and more demanding as she takes on the role of gallery manager. A new assistant is hired to handle the books, freeing Amber to interview more local artists. She wants to add some of their work to the gallery's display space, especially smaller pieces, just right for tourists to take home in a suitcase.

Jim comes by every few days, sometimes bringing a lunch to share. One day he arrives with a large painting he has just completed. He assumes the gallery will display it in the same space as his previous large painting, the sailboat and Mt. Baker.

"Uh, have you finished any more of your paintings combining natural beauty and surrealism?" Amber asks. She can see that the painting, a pictorial of the Boat Show, is not good art. She knows he can do better.

Jim shakes his head. "I've hit a dry spot."

"I'm sorry, but I can't accept this painting." She reaches out and holds his hand. "It's okay. You have a treasure cove of good art in you, you just need to do it."

"Thanks," he says and leaves, taking the painting with him.

Amber realizes that once again, he has not mentioned painting her. She wonders if he ever will.

Two days later, Jim comes to the gallery with a paper wrapped package for Amber. She opens it, and says, "A poem, how nice, and beautifully framed. Did you write this? When?"

"Well…ah…," says Jim. "I started writing after that first day we met, hoping to capture some of my thoughts and feelings. It's framed for sale."

"Yes, of course," she says. "It's, it's... You do like triangles, don't you? The words... 'The Touching.' Thank you."

Feeling less flustered after Jim leaves, Amber reads the poem.

THE TOUCHING

I am looking at you, time stands still, images racing
I want to touch your face. I need to know.
My face is touched....I stand up
My padded coat falls off
I am...emerging
Lips Touch
OH
!
Fusing
Blending
Combining
Commingling.
The core of a vortex
a thousand light years across
The center of a vast, beautiful galaxy
Colors I have never seen, sounds never heard
A swirl of energy, vibrating, spinning, humming, tones
Arms surround, embrace, holding, caressing, merging,
touching.

As the date for the Boat Festival approaches, the whole town becomes energized. Even businesses that have nothing to do with boats spruce up their shops.

Amber finds an apartment near the gallery. The previous tenant was desperate to leave Port Townsend before the "hordes" (as he called them) descended on the town and before he had to endure another Northwest winter.

So much the better for me, thinks Amber. Another example of things working out for me without my pushing too hard.

The bell on the gallery door announces a visitor. The jingle seems so old fashioned, but its pleasant call is definitely better than an electric buzzer. Amber had noticed a young man dressed in expensive-looking yachting clothes looking in the window. She is more excited by the boat show than she realized. She hopes the new visitor won't stay too long, but business ....

"Hi," says the man, flashing a captivating smile. He takes a few steps towards her.

She realizes he's been watching her.

"You have some beautiful work here," says the man. "Are they local artists? I mean Northwest..." His eyes take in the words on the sign she's holding.

See you at the Boat Festival

Have a great time!

Back at 2:30

"Oh, you're trying to close."

Amber smiles. "Well, yes. But that's ok. Take your time."

"I was on my way to the show," says the man, "when I noticed your beautiful art, just checking it out, you know, to come back later."

"Thanks, you should definitely come back," says Amber.

"I certainly will," says the man. "I like the painting of the girl on the deck of the sailboat. Do I need to put a hold on it?"

"Done," says Amber. "It's by one of our local artists."

How right she'd been not to accept Jim's large painting, and just a few days ago he'd brought in this impressive smaller canvas. He was pleased when she made room for it in the window.

"Since we're both going to the festival, can we walk together?" asks the man. "I would like a local to show me the ropes...no pun intended."

Amber nods. This guy is charming. She can't quite place his accent, interesting. "Yes," she says. "I hear it's quite a performance. I hope the boats remember their lines."

"Uh-oh, I can't match that," says the man. "You're great."

"Thanks, but I'm not even a local."

"Really?" asks the man, "How long have you lived here?"

"About five weeks," she says. "I'm very curious. I'm really excited to see so many beautiful boats. Let's go!"

"Here, let me help. I'll hold the sign while you tape it. By the way, I'm Paul."

"Thanks, Paul. I'm Amber."

As she closes the door behind them, their eyes meet for a moment.

As they walk to the harbor, they're both thinking about what to say.

"So, what brought you to Port Townsend?"

"I was just getting ready to ask you the same question."

"You first."

"I bet the answers are similar."

"Like, tired of the rat race..."

"And looking for a ..."

"Beautiful place to work and..."

"Settle. And finding..."

Paul and Amber stop, look at each other, knowing what the next line would be, but afraid to say it out loud.

"Let's not forget the Boat Festival," says Amber. "After all, isn't that what we're here for today?"

"Yes, you're right," says Paul. "But I would like to continue our conversation."

"We will."

They stop on the street above the harbor.

"I've never seen so many boats," says Amber. "And they're all so beautiful."

"I've seen yacht harbors filled with boats, in Southern California," says Paul. "But this is different. These boats are all made of wood. And that makes them more alive."

"Ah, so that's why it's called the WOODEN Boat Festival. I didn't realize, but they do seem to be more beautiful," says Amber.

They look out over the show, taking it all in. Amber searches for Jim's boat. It's not there. She remembers that he had to relocate *Amber* to another harbor, making room for show boats. Sure enough, when she locates Jim's moorage spot, there are three small sailboats tied closely together in his space. She has only seen him once since he brought in the large painting. She had been relieved when he dropped off the smaller painting. A feeling of concern for Jim floods her mind.

Paul interrupts her thoughts, "Let's go down to get a closer look."

The docks are crowded, Amber reaches out and holds onto Paul's arm when they meet a large, boisterous group on the narrow dock. It seems very natural to let her hand slip down and take his hand in hers. It's warm, and Paul gives her hand a little squeeze. He looks at her with a smile.

"I'd like to walk over and check out that two-masted boat on the next dock."

"Sure, it really looks beautiful. They all do. I think this should be called the 'Beautiful Wooden Boat Festival,'" says Amber as they cross over to the next dock.

"Hi, is this your boat?" Paul asks the man sitting in the cockpit.

"Yes," comes the answer. "I built it myself."

"Oh, wow," says Paul. "It's beautiful!"

"Thanks."

"How long did it take?" asks Amber.

The man laughs. "That's the first question everyone asks. Two years, maybe two and a half. I'm retired and always wanted to build my own boat. My kids helped when they could."

"I'd love to build a boat," says Paul. "But—"

"Takes time and long-term commitment," says the man. "Like raising a child. You have a kid?"

"Not yet," answers Paul, glancing at Amber who is studying the beautiful woodworking on the boat's railing.

She does not see his glance.

"My advice," says the man. "Get a wooden boat that you really like and see if you enjoy puttering on it. Wish we could do the same with kids, both take a lot of work."

A group of people joins them on the dock. The man turns to answer a question. More people crowd in, pushing Paul and Amber back.

"This is too crowded," Paul says. "Let's go look at the other boats in the parking lot."

"Sounds good to me," Amber says. "And I see some food stands. I'm hungry."

The young couple is separated by the press of people squeezing up the dock ramp. The hoards are here, thinks Amber. But they're just happy people enjoying the beauty of the boats.

"Look," says Paul. "They're selling corn on the cob. I would love some. How about you?"

"Yes!" Amber says. "It may sound corny, but I don't think it will ruin my appetite for a real lunch."

"Ha! I'm not going there," says Paul.

A beautiful white-haired woman serves them two hot buttered ears of corn with a warm smile. Paul asks if she grew the corn herself.

"Oh, no," she answers. "But we're supplied by a local farmer. It was harvested this morning."

"Er, um," says Amber, looking up at Paul, "You have some corn in your beard."

"Oh, sorry. Thanks." He tries to wipe the kernels away with a paper towel.

"Here," says Amber. "Let me." She moves in closer, takes the towel, and gently removes the errant kernels. Paul feels the gentle touch of her hand on his beard. He looks into Amber's face, her brown eyes glow in the sunlight. He sees the complex colors, not only brown, but greens and golds and reds.

"My god!" exclaims Paul. "Your eyes are amber…I have a piece of stone…a gem…it's my favorite."

"Thanks, not many people see that. I guess most people don't get close enough."

Paul thinks, did she just move in closer or was that me? He can feel the warmth of her body pressing. They turn and walk hand in hand to the dry land boat show in the parking lot.

At the edge of the lot a few people are selling crafts, food and whatever from their trucks.

"Oh, there's Jim," says Amber. "I want you to meet him. He's the artist that created the painting that caught your eye."

They walk over to where Jim stands, his large painting arranged on an easel next to his truck.

"Hi, I'm Paul. I really like your painting of the girl on the deck of a sailboat."

"Thanks," says Jim.

"I'm intrigued by your use of triangles. On the main sail behind the girl, the stitching reads as triangles. So does the three-sided jib fore sail. Is the girl going forward to tend to the head sail? The way she's standing or walking on the slopping deck, reaching out to hold the safety cable is also a triangle. Her body, her arm, and the line she holds form the three sides. And there in the distance is the beautiful, snow-covered triangular mountain. It's just magnificent."

"You got it," says Jim. "Not many people do."

"Oh, I do," says Paul. "I'm fascinated by triangles. I love to study fractals. You know, triangles, within triangles, within…"

"Yeah, me too," says Jim. "But fractals are pretty boring to paint. I like to show what I see around me. They're all around, everywhere, everything is made of triangles."

"Even the mountain," Paul says. "What's its name? Or is it your fantasy? And who is the girl?"

Jim shakes his head. "No, that's Mt. Baker." He steals a quick glance at Amber. "I don't know who she is."

"It's just beautiful. I know as I live with the painting, I will see more," says Paul.

"Do you sail?" asks Jim.

"Yes," says Paul.

"Do you have a —" Jim starts to ask.

Paul interrupts him. "Is this your painting of the boat show? It's a very large canvas."

"Yes, and I hope someone will buy it."

"It's very colorful," Paul says. "You've certainly captured the party spirit of the boat show. Is it always this crowded?" He turns and places his hand on Amber's waist. "We need to go."

Jim scowls and turns away. "Yeah," he mumbles over his shoulder. "It's always crowded."

As soon as they're out of Jim's hearing, Amber turns to Paul. "Why did you interrupt Jim's line of questioning?"

Paul kicks a loose stone in the path. "I hate it when people ask how big your boat is. It's like asking how much money you make. Or how big your…well, you know. It's a value judgement. I don't like it. As soon as I said I had a boat, that was going to be his next question."

"Jim is sweet," says Amber. "I don't think he meant any harm."

"Maybe you're right," says Paul. "I like him and really respect his talent to see the world around him."

The couple meanders through the collection of small boats; many have raised sails. All are on trailers. Approaching the end, Amber says. "Look at that one! It's the most beautiful boat I've ever seen. It's different from all these others."

"You're right," says Paul. "Beautiful."

An old man dressed in bib overalls sits on a folding camp chair next to the boat. He has white hair and a long beard.

"I bet he's a local," whispers Paul to Amber.

The man looks up as Amber says, "Hello, is this your boat? Did you build it? What kind of boat is it?"

"Yes and no," comes the answer. "It's a Terrik, plans by Ian Ouchtred, a Scottish designer and builder. A friend built it years ago, but I've kept it repaired. It takes a lot of loving care to keep a wooden boat in good shape. But I love the work."

"You've done a great job," says Paul. "Why is the name along the side? I've never seen that on a boat."

"I'm Amber and this is Paul."

"Hi, I'm Roger. The name's on the side, 'cause this is a double ender with no flat transom in the back for a name."

"Looks a little like a Viking ship. Is it fast?" says Amber.

"Fast enough," says Roger. "But it's very seaworthy, like the old Viking designs. And she's easy to row."

"You call the boat 'she', but the name on the side is a man's."

"Right," says Roger. "In the old maritime tradition, a ship, a vessel was often named after the original owner, so, the name *Welton R.*"

"That's kinda like artists signing their work, their creation," says Amber. "How come you have his boat?"

"We were friends for more than forty years, sailing buddies, then he got too old to sail. He used a walker, then a wheelchair. Gave me his beloved boat." Roger sighs. "I did some needed repairs and renamed it." He continues with a quaver in his voice, "Now *I'm* getting too old…."

"So now you're selling, moving the boat on…" says Paul. "Letting go…"

"But it has to go to the right person," insists Roger.

"Of course," says Paul. "I would love to have it."

Amber turns to Paul with raised eyebrows. "Really?" she exclaims. "I didn't know you were so spontaneous."

"There's a lot you don't know about me," Paul says. "I hope you'll—"

He turns to the older man and explains that he only arrived last night, mainly to visit the festival, but was also looking for the right place to live, and maybe, someday owning a wooden sailboat. Paul looks over at the Terrik again and laughs. "Seems like the sequence has become turned around. Someday is already here."

Roger asks, "What does your lovely lady have to say about—?"

"Oh, we're not a couple," says Paul, "I just met her an hour ago."

"I'm the new art gallery director," says Amber. "He stopped in to look at a painting on his way to the show."

"Hum, could'a fooled me," says Roger. "Here's my phone number. If you decide to settle here, give me a call. I'll take you for a spin and if you can sail and if you fit, then maybe I'll sell her to you."

"Oh, thanks," says Paul. "I just don't know…"

"And if you two are still together," says Roger to Amber. "You come too."

Amber checks her watch. "Oh, my God! I've got to get back to work. Thanks so much, Roger. I would love to talk with you again. Please come by the gallery."

"Will do."

The "couple" walks quickly towards the exit. "Paul, you can stay at the show. You don't have to come back to the gallery. I'll hold the—"

"Nope, I'm coming," says Paul. "I'll come back to the boat show tomorrow, if…and I want to look at the painting."

Back at the gallery, Amber moves the canvas to where Paul can view it from across the room or close up. She also sees the artwork from a new perspective. The sailboat is Jim's, which makes sense. But who is the woman on the boat's deck? The red/gold hair looks like hers. Could it be? But without seeing the face… and Jim said he painted it months ago.

"Okay, I'll take it," says Paul. "Here's my credit card. Can you keep it for me? My motel room's not—"

"Of course, no hurry."

"Shall we celebrate over dinner tonight?" asks Paul.

"I'd love to, but I'm pretty tired, and I think all the restaurants will be jammed packed," says Amber.

"We both have to eat. You close at five-thirty? I'll be back at that time and we'll figure out a plan," says Paul. "See you in a bit."

Amber makes sure all the gallery lights are on and sits at her desk in the back with its light off. She begins her meditation, knowing that "one ear" is open to hear the jingle of the door. The sequences of the day go through her mind. Meeting Paul by chance, or was that synchronicity? And the observation that— what's his name?—Roger, made of them being a couple.

The meditation comes to an end on its own. Looking out, Amber sees the few people returning from the festival are too tired or preoccupied to even look in the gallery windows. Deciding to close early, she tapes a note with her phone number on the door for Paul.

He calls exactly at five-thirty. Amber comes right to the point. They both have to eat. She has a BBQ on her patio, complete with fuel, which she hasn't used yet. Could he pick up a couple of steaks and a bottle of wine (his choice)? She has salad makings in her fridge. And also, she has two potatoes that could be baked. They could be done by six-thirty or seven. Oh yes, if he wants sour cream on his potato, please bring some. She has butter.

"Sounds great," says Paul, finally getting a word in edgewise. "I had envisioned a quiet dinner with candlelight, etcetera, but this sounds like a relaxed, fun evening. See you about seven. What's the dress code for—?"

"Tux with tails," says Amber. "Definitely T and T."

"Sounds great," he says. "Just like prom."

"Ugh, I hope not." Amber laughs. "Just casual. Do you have something besides your yachting garb? Like jeans?"

"Sounds even better."

He hangs up before she can respond.

Amber moves about, getting ready. She's constantly surprised by how much stuff the former tenant left behind. He was so happy to break his lease without penalty, he sold everything in the apartment to her for a few hundred dollars. She opens a drawer and finds two beautiful, tapered candles. Tablecloths are nonexistent, so far.

Amber is just brushing her hair when Paul knocks.

"Wow, what a great apartment," he says, coming in.

"Thanks," she replies. "And I haven't even moved in. I've only been here a week."

"Then how did you get all this …?"

"It's from The Universal Abundance," says Amber, explaining the deal she made with the former tenant.

"Humm, do you really believe that?" says Paul. "I mean about the abundance and all?"

"You bet," she says. "Very much so."

"We have to talk about that sometime," he says. "I'm very curious what your take is on the subject."

Amber steps forward and touches Paul's arm.

"I would like that," she says. "But now I'm really hungry. Did the universe bring dinner?"

"No," says Paul. "I did. But maybe I'm just the messenger."

Paul opens the wine and sets it on the table. Finding the candles laying down, he melts a little wax and sets them upright on saucers. "Ah, dinner by candlelight. Just what I wanted."

"Salad's ready," says Amber. "Will you bring the steaks? I'll get the potatoes from the oven."

"Sounds good to me," Paul says.

During dinner they share family history, experiences both sad and humorous, and of course recall the boat show. Paul asks Amber about her beliefs in The Universal Abundance.

She sets down her fork and looks intently at him. "I'd rather not talk about it," she says. "At least not now."

"Okay, but why not?" he asks.

"That's talking about it," she says and laughs.

"Yeah, sorry, you're right," he says.

Amber stands up and starts to clear. Paul jumps up to help. She turns, still holding two plates, and says to him, "After cleanup, let's sit on the couch. I'll tell you."

They sit awkwardly on the couch next to each other. Amber slides back into the corner. Kicking off her shoes, she lifts one knee up. He follows, also pulling one knee up. Their feet touch.

"The reason I'm hesitant to talk, to open up," she says, "is most people, even friends, are not able to listen to what I believe, what I know."

"I understand," he says. "It's like they can't imagine something so very different from their tried-and-true beliefs."

"Right," she says. "Or they try to understand, and the only way they can is to cut and paste my beliefs to fit into the parameters of their system or their own worldview. What's left is not what I know."

"Sounds pretty difficult," says Paul. "Sometimes, words just don't have what it takes to communicate. But what else do we have?"

"Occasionally, art can communicate where words can't," Amber says. "Like your new painting. There's definitely something being said about triangles, but what?"

Paul laughs and shifts himself closer to Amber. "I'm looking forward to joining the woman on the boat to see where it takes me. I wonder who's at the helm. Who has their hand on the tiller."

"You seem to be able steer the course," says Amber, reaching over and touching Paul's arm.

"Humm, thanks. I hope so. But back to you and your Universal Abundance."

"I'll try to condense, but that seems like cutting and —"

"Please," says Paul. "Don't cut corners to make it fit into the parameters and limitations of a single evening on a couch. We might just have to meet again and ..."

He takes her hand and touches it to his lips, then tries to pull her to him.

Amber jumps up, reaches out, pulls Paul up and off his seat. "Sounds good to me," she says. "But not tonight. It's late and I have a big day at work tomorrow." Still holding his hand, she gives Paul a kiss on the cheek, and pulls him to the door.

"I'll see you tomorrow," says Paul. "And we'll talk more about Abundance. Goodnight. It was a great day,"

"It definitely was," says Amber. "Go to the boat festival and look at— what was the name, something *R*—and talk with Roger. I bet he knows the area and might help you find what you're looking for."

"Hi, Roger," says Paul. "I was here yesterday, looking…"

"Oh yes," says Roger. "With that charming woman. Where is she?"

"She's at the gallery, hoping to make some sales with the festival crowd. I came by to look at your boat again and ask some questions. Tell me about the design, and would it be a practical boat for here in the Northwest?"

"Good," says Roger. "I'm about ready to pack up and head for home. I'm not much of a salesman when it comes to parting with… I mean, selling this boat."

"Sounds like saying 'goodbye' to a friend," says Paul.

Roger recounts his affection for the boat, its unique design, and the craftsmanship. He points out the two bronze rub rails on the bottom. "It was designed to be sailed right up on a sandy beach." He continues relating his forty-plus-year friendship with the builder, and how hard it was at the end. "As far as this being a good boat for this area," he says. "Yes and no. If you want to cruise, it's too small. But it trailers easily, which opens access to a vast playground up here." He stops, lost in memories. "I wish I'd done more."

"Sounds good to me," says Paul. "I'd love to gunk hole but haven't done much."

"Why not?"

"My boat's too big."

The two men continue talking boats, the ease of setting up a small boat and being able to row if there is no wind.

"Oh well," says Roger. "I'm going up to get my truck. On the way, I'm stopping to get a corn on the cob. Do you want to join me?"

The two men sit on a bench enjoying their corn, getting some in their beards. They seem oblivious to the boat show babble around them.

"I like you," says Roger. "Do you want the boat?"

"Phew, *YES!*" says Paul. "Like I said yesterday, the last thing on my list seems to come to me first. But—"

"Oh hell," says Roger. "That's easy…Follow your bliss. It's gotten you this far already. Go for it! I know a good realtor. She'll find you the perfect place."

"Will you take a check for the boat?" asks Paul.

"Naw," says Roger. "The boat's yours. Find a place with a double garage. You'll need it. One needs a workshop in the winters up here. I'll keep the boat safe for you. Pay me when you're ready."

"Thanks," says Paul. "Here's a check, I insist."

Roger stuffs the check in the front of his overalls without looking at it. "Wait a minute," he says. "The realtor's office is near the gallery. You ready to go? I'll give her a call."

She picks up right away. "Hi Amy, Roger here. I got a friend looking for the perfect place. You have the time? Good, he'll be there in fifteen or twenty. Thanks."

Roger jumps up, grabs Paul's hand. "Go for it! Now all you need is a job."

"That I have," says Paul. "Thanks. Keep my boat safe. Oh, I'll need some lessons on rigging, and you know…"

"Okay, okay," says Roger. "I'm so happy to have found you."

Paul walks briskly up the street. He's so excited he feels like running. He decides to stop at the gallery, just to say "Hi" and share his excitement.

At the gallery, Amber smiles, recalling the evening with Paul. She liked his touching her, maybe more the next time. Since the gallery's empty, she contemplates closing for lunch. It's been a long time since her morning coffee and scone. The doorbell jingles and Jim rushes over to her. "I'm so excited, I wanted to celebrate with you! I sold the big painting!"

"That's wonderful! But I'm starving," says Amber. "How about having lunch with me? Could you go for sandwiches? I'll buy."

"Nope," says Jim. "I'll buy. My treat."

Just as Jim is leaving, Amber sees Paul wave from the street. But he doesn't come in.

She wonders if Paul saw Jim and turned away. No, Paul likes Jim, or at least his painting. Maybe it's a guy thing, Wow! She thinks. I've been here less than two months, and already three men are interested in me.

Amber goes to the deli almost every day for lunch, and the young owner is obviously interested in her. She knows it would never work. His religious beliefs are so strong, what she knows would have to be cut and pasted to fit into the parameters of his worldview. For her, what she knows is more than a belief, it's a knowing. A knowing that she has experienced many times in daily life, a vital part of her being, a familiar part of her life.

Jim returns with lunch, including chips and apple juice.

"The owner said this was your favorite beverage. I think he likes you."

They spread the lunch out on her desk in the back of the

gallery. Amber sits where she can see the front door. Jim's different than usual, she thinks. He was, of course, very pleased with the sale of his two paintings. But there's something else.

"What's on your mind?" she asks.

"Ah, um, thanks for asking." Jim explains that he needs to bring his boat back to his moorage after the festival ends tomorrow. Could she go with him to the boat, go for a sail, then give him a ride back to get his truck? Amber agrees, ready for a day off. When a potential customer comes in, Jim leaves with a smile on his face.

Amber's phone chimes, announcing a text.

> Hi, Paul here. Saw you
> were busy. Bought the
> boat. Was at Realtor
> looking for a house. Got
> work call. I'll be away for
> a few weeks. See you.

Amber's heart thumps a flip-flop. What does he mean? Does Paul really want to move to Port Townsend? He said he bought the boat and was looking for a place. But why is he going to be away for so long? Is there another woman stashed somewhere? What work? He never said what he does. Most men love to talk about their work.

She glances over at the painting Paul left in her care and wonders what to do with it. It's hung on the display wall with a red dot on the card below. Well, it's good advertising.

On the drive to his boat, Jim is quiet. At the moorage, he asks Amber if she can handle the dock lines. She gives him a thumbs up, and releases the spring lines. He goes aboard, starts the diesel engine; she coils and stows the lines. Walking beside the boat as it slowly backs along the finger pier, she sees Jim smiling.

"Cast Off!" shouts Jim above the engine noise.

"Aye, aye sir!" Amber shouts back. She smiles; both shouts were louder than needed to be heard above the engine, but it was fun.

Aboard and settling in the cockpit, Jim hands Amber a life jacket. "Better put this on." He slips into his own jacket.

Amber has sailed before, but never in a boat of this size. She watches as Jim turns into the wind, throttles down, raises the main sail, and unfurls the rolled-up head sail. The engine is shut down, the wind fills the sails, and the boat *Amber* comes alive. The woman Amber also is enlivened. The wind and waves play their energies on the sails, hull, and her. It is a feeling like no other. There is a humming in the very core of her body as it adjusts to the rolling and heeling of the boat. She's a part of, an extension of, the boat.

She looks back at Jim, his legs in a sturdy, supporting stance, holding the wheel, his face in the wind. He is in his world, captain of his ship. Their eyes meet. They smile.

Looking forward, Amber notices one of the mooring lines dragging in the water. She stands up, snaps to the safety line and goes forward, her body adapting to the movement of the deck. She is at one with the boat, the waves, and the wind. This is also her world.

There are triangles everywhere; in the corner stitching of the sails, the sails themselves, and the standing rigging supporting the mast. Even the mooring line forms a triangle as she pulls it in. Stepping forward to secure the coiled line, she looks out around the head sail, beyond the forestay.

"Oh, my God!" she utters. Mt. Baker is before her in all its beauty. A bright, white triangle floating just above the horizon's thin line of dark forests. The waters of Puget Sound stretch out before her to the mountain, to infinity.

The beauty, the experience of wind and waves, the feeling… it's too much for her small body to contain, to encompass. She moves above, expanding, filling the whole view, looking down at the boat, the mountain, and at herself. She is at one with everything. She is everything, the wind, the water, even the mountain in the distance, and all between. Her eyes fill with tears of joy, then blink.

She is standing in front of an art gallery looking in the window at a large painting of a sailboat, and in the distance is a white, triangular mountain. Pressing her face against the window glass, she sees the woman with red/gold hair standing on the boat's deck looking back at her. They both smile. She hears herself say, "Maybe I should buy this painting, even before I find a place to live."

Returning to her view above the boat, everything has shifted. The triangle shaped mountain is closer. The sailboat is much larger, so large the dimensions are beyond the borders. Some of the boat, and part of the sail, are beyond her view, outside her awareness. There is a woman standing on the deck. It is herself. Amber's view from above becomes a painting, the composition is triangles within triangles within triangles. It is a fractal.

The boat hits a tall wave, the wake from a large power boat. The thump travels through Amber, connecting her back into her body standing on the boat deck.

"Thanks for stowing the line," says Jim. "You looked very natural out there on the foredeck. Having fun?"

"Yes, but I need to get back."

"No problem," says Jim. "We're just at the entrance to the harbor. Be ashore in fifteen."

Amber stands at the bow, mooring line in hand. She watches as Jim executes the difficult maneuver of turning his large boat around in the narrow space between docks. He gently lays *Amber* alongside his moorage space. She steps off and helps tie the lines to the cleats on the dock.

They walk up the ramp towards his truck.

"Before you go, I would like to show you something. It's over here on the bench," Jim says.

"Isn't this the bench I sat on that first day?" asks Amber. "You know, when I felt my grandpa's presence."

"Yes, seems like it's a special place.

They sit, and Jim begins to talk. A few days before the boat show, after she didn't accept his large painting, he was feeling really low. He'd thought the wall space was his. He had completed the large canvas which, as she knows, large canvas equals large dollars. He was grateful she'd accepted his small painting, even though it was a much older work. Maybe eight months, or a year old. But now he thought of himself as a large-scale artist. When he returned from moving *Amber* for the show, he was in the pits. No boat to go to, close the hatch, and roll up in his sleeping bag.

"I know this is getting long, but I really…"

"No, no," Amber says. "Go on, I want to hear."

Jim continues. He went out and set on this bench, had a little cry, and started thinking about his uncle. Joe, his uncle, had been like a father to him. He had put the first paint brush in Jim's hands, said it was okay to use his left hand. He taught him and encouraged him to keep painting. Joe loved horses and produced beautiful portraits. One day, Joe gave Jim a pin, a brooch with the stylized image of a horse head. Jim thought it was a girl's pin, but Joe insisted it was special. After Joe died, Jim kept the pin near the amber touchstone on his boat.

Jim pauses, looks down at his boat in the harbor below. Amber can tell that he's struggling. He looks up at her and says, "Look at the table. Tell me what you see."

"Not much."

"Look again, up close, right there in front of you."

"Well, I see… oh, my God! There's a horse head. Did you carve this? It looks old, the cut lines are dark, filled with dirt."

"No, it appeared, at least I first saw it, while I was thinking about my Uncle Joe. I felt his presence. He was here, talking with me, encouraging me to keep painting. That my paintings would sell." Jim starts to laugh, releasing some deep feelings. "He told me to stop painting crap, to paint what I know."

"I guess I was right not displaying your large canvas," says Amber. "It was hard saying 'no' to you. But I knew you could do better, like the one with all the triangles."

"And it sold, too, the day you put it in the window." Jim leans forward, elbows on the table, clenches his fists, and looks across the table at Amber. She holds his gaze, reaches out and takes his fists in her hands.

"What is it?" she asks.

Jim relaxes, opens his fists, but continues to hold her hands. "What is it. I mean, how…? I've thought of Uncle Joe before, but never like this."

"Pretty special, isn't it," says Amber.

"Yeah, maybe even awesome."

Amber can feel Jim trembling. "That's because you were, and even now are, feeling awe."

Jim tries to pull away, but Amber grips his hands.

"Stay here…stay with it," she says.

"But I just don't understand." Jim says. "How…?"

"You're trying to define the undefinable," she says. "We have nothing in our physical world, or in our language, to explain what happened."

"But…"

"I know," says Amber. "Every explanation ends with an exasperated, 'Yes, but…' and a person is left with an uneasy question. I guess it comes down to one's personal belief."

"Well," asks Jim, "what do you believe?"

"To even begin to understand," she says, "you need to suspend your disbeliefs, otherwise, everything I say will automatically filter through what you believe."

Using Jim's recent experience of connecting with his Uncle Joe, Amber explains that we live in (at least) two worlds. One, the physical world we are all familiar with. We perceive it through our senses. It is the favorite playground of scientists and engineers. It is contained within the borders of physical space and the flow of time. Within these boundaries, the limits, there are unlimited opportunities to explore, measure, define, etc.

The other world, the non-physical, is not limited or restricted by space/time. There are no borders. It's hard to comprehend, because we have no language or experience to relate this world to, unless, one has had a first-hand experience of the nonphysical.

"You, Jim," Amber says, "have had just such an experience. Your Uncle Joe is in the other world. He is not restricted by time. Joe can move, in what we call forward and back, in our time. He can place the carving of the horse, the subject dear to you both, on the table where he knows you will see it when you need it. Finding the carving makes it possible for you to know he is near. You don't just believe it, you know it."

Jim nods in agreement.

"Beliefs can be modified, filtered, distorted, changed, and manipulated. Knowing is from personal experience, like with

Uncle Joe. You have received a very special gift. You'll always know he's near. He'll continue encouraging you to paint what you know."

Amber is tempted to tell Jim of her own shifting from one reality to another while on his boat this morning. She decides not to. He has enough of his own experience to integrate into his worldview.

Jim stands up, walks around the bench. Amber stands, and he embraces her. "Thank you. I love you for trusting, for sharing this intimate place with me. Sometimes I think you're my touchstone, giving me direction."

In the weeks to come, the two spend more and more time together, on his boat and at her place. The evenings often end with a long embrace, neither knowing how far to take the intimacy.

Roger, wearing his signature bib overalls, comes by the gallery one afternoon when Jim's there with Amber. "Have either of you seen or heard from Paul?" the older man asks.

Both shake their heads.

"I just came from my realtor friend, neither has she," says Roger. "I'm concerned. His check for the boat cleared, but when I sent a receipt, the letter came back, no one at that address, and no forwarding."

"That's very strange," says Amber. "The credit card charge for the painting went through. He texted me that he was called away for work, but I haven't heard from him since."

"What kind of work?" Jim asks.

Amber shrugs. "He never said."

"So, I wonder what to do with the boat?" says Roger. "I didn't expect to keep a boat inside through the winter taking up shop space. Then again, with what he paid me... I know! I'll build a carport, or rather a boatport, next to my shop."

"I'll text him," Amber says. She tries a few times, but the text won't go through. "Weird."

"It's like he's fallen into a hole in the space/time continuum," Roger says.

Jim laughs. "Maybe he disappeared into the dark underground."

"He didn't seem like a gangster," says Amber. "Could he be in some kind of trouble?"

Roger strokes his white beard. "Let's give it some time and see if he turns up."

"I'll keep the painting on the gallery wall," says Amber. "Looks good to have a 'sold' red dot on the tag."

Jim smiles. "So, you finally have one of my paintings."

Roger studies the new painting until Jim leaves. He turns to Amber and asks, "Are you an avatar?"

"Why? I've never been asked that before. What's an avatar?"

"A deity or spirit that alights and takes on the material essence of a human," says Roger. "Comes from the Hindu faith, but you don't have to be a Hindu to be an avatar."

"Why me?"

"Well, you have red hair—"

"Red-gold."

"Coulda fooled me. Tradition has it that avatars, these helpers, have red hair," says Roger.

"Have you ever met an avatar?" Amber asks with a grin.

"Yeah, my girlfriend had red hair before we met. Now her hair is white. She came to me a year or so after my wife crossed over and brought me love and joy and feminine energy."

"How do you know she's an avatar?"

"I just know. She came at a time of my need," Roger says. "She helped me get back on track."

Amber reaches over and takes Roger's hand. "I'd love to meet her."

"You already have. She was selling corn at the festival. These avatars arrive as helpers, and you certainly have guided and helped Jim."

Amber squeezes Roger's hand, gives him a long look, a warm smile on her lips. Just as she's about to speak, the doorbell chimes.

Roger holds her hand tighter. "You haven't answered my question."

She glances at the front door, leans into Roger and gives him a kiss on the cheek.

My God she smells good, Roger thinks. I'm sure she's an avatar.

With a grin, she says "I will." She turns, walks to the front of the gallery.

The next day, Amber receives a letter at the art gallery, postmarked from Switzerland. The address doesn't even have the gallery's name. It just says: "Art Gallery near Boat Harbor, Port Townsend, Washington State, USA."

The letter is just as cryptic:

To Whom it may Concern.

Please hang the painting on your wall with "sold" sign.

I will not be returning.

P.

The second page is a sheet of paper torn from a school notebook. The hastily scribbled pencil is difficult to decipher. Amber makes out something about a friend mailing the letter, and if safe, adding this note. "I'm sorry not to have told you earlier, but the call came unexpectedly. A business connection with a rebel group in a third world country. I thought the job was finished. It wasn't. Now I'm here."

Amber struggles to read the words written in the fold of the note paper in smudged pencil.

"Also, I met up with an old lover from the other side. She claims her son is mine. I must be very careful. Both sides want me dead. I'm trying to do the right thing. As much as possible my identity has been deleted. Please burn this letter"

Amber's hands shake. All her darkest fantasies are true or worse. She's glad she sent him away that night, that she listened to herself. If she had become deeply involved with Paul... And just what *is* his business? Guns? Drugs? Thank goodness, it pulled him away when it did. If they had had another date, she might have... She shudders at the thought. Burning the letter is a relief.

As the days pass, Amber is pleased that her memories of Paul fade quickly. When she looks at the painting on the wall, she sees herself on Jim's boat, looking at herself looking at the painting and recognizing herself on the boat. It is a good feeling.

Amber invites Jim for dinner at her place. Steak, baked potato, and salad, making her wonder briefly if this evening is a replay, in some way, of that earlier time spent with Paul. After dinner, they sit on the couch, their bare feet touching.

"I like playing footsie with you," says Jim.

"Oh no, don't tell me you have a foot fetish."

"Yep," says Jim. "And every other part of a woman's body, too."

Amber laughs and moving forward, gives him a kiss. "I like that," she says, turning and leaning against him.

Jim puts his arm around her. "This feels very comfortable."

"Yes, it does."

They sit together in peaceful silence for a while. Amber sits up, looking at Jim, tells him of her experience on his boat. She includes "going back in time" and observing herself viewing the paintings through the gallery window.

"I recognized myself on *Amber*, in the painting you painted before we met." She sighs. "That all happened the day you told me about the horse head carving on the bench. I guess I had my own experience of, of, well, of time travel."

Jim gives her a hug. "It's very exciting exploring and sharing this new dimension together."

They kiss. Amber pulls Jim up from the couch and leads him to her bedroom. She undresses layer by layer in the soft light of the bedside lamp. Lying flat on the bed, she extends her hand to welcome Jim.

Jim remains rooted to the floor, taking in the profound beauty before him. Amber rolls over, presenting her beautiful back side to his view.

He sits on the edge of the bed and reaches over to caress the side of her face. His hand, his left hand, moves down her back, over her hips, and on down. The fingers recording every curve and texture of her body. The complex colors of the skin, the light and dark, constantly changing as she breaths, all is imprinted in his brain, in his psyche.

The image of Galatea flashes across his mind and disappears. Here before him is pure beauty, warm, soft, with no vestige of marble.

"I will paint this," says Jim.

"Of course you will." Amber laughs. "Take your clothes off and come here. I'm getting cold."

The next morning, over breakfast, Amber begins telling Jim of her thoughts about triangles. She had seen an OpEd in the newspaper about the power and stability (if each side held their part) of the triangle between China, Russia, and the U.S. Of course, the U.S. was on the bottom, the place of stability, holding the other sides in place. She had toyed with the possibility of there being a triangle of herself (on the bottom, of course) with Paul and Jim.

Now, with Paul's disappearance, one side of the triangle has been removed.

"And the triangle collapses," says Amber.

"And a side falls down, laying next to the—" says Jim.

"Making wild, beautiful love," Amber says with a laugh.

After breakfast, the couple takes their coffee out to the patio. The sun is shining, but the breeze is cool. Amber slips her padded coat over her shoulders. It promises to be one of the beautiful, fall days that the Pacific Northwest is known for. They sit on a bench.

Jim breaks into her thoughts. "I suspected, but never knew for sure, that you and Paul were an item."

"We were not," says Amber. "But I did like him. There was a bright spark between us, but it never burst into flame."

"Do you think our flame will last?" asks Jim.

"I'm not sure... yes, probably," says Amber. "I guess the winds of time will either blow out the flame, or fan the very bright spark into a roaring, white-hot love."

Jim stands, pulls Amber up. She lifts her face to him. He touches her face with his left hand.

Her padded coat falls away.

THE MIRROR

They said it couldn't be done. And they were 100% right… if, and that is a big "if," one is satisfied (I was going to say "stuck") with the Newtonian definition of the physical world. His laws assume that distance, time, and mass, are absolute.

But I knew there was something, some being, some "whatever", on the other side. I was told there was no way to make it through the wall, it was solid glass. Some even said it might as well be hundreds, even thousands, of feet thick. But I knew there was a way. This was no ordinary glass. This was no "seeing as through a glass darkly" quality. It was a mirror.

I was obsessed by my knowing. Looking for others who could understand and growing angry when they belittled the subject. I was unable to rationalize it away or accept it and go on. I knew the "something" was vital to my existence.

Standing back and looking in the mirror, only myself and all the shapes behind me are in view. Putting my face up close and cupping my hands, I try to look through but see only the reflection of my eyeball. There is no sound or smell. However, when I put my hand flat on the surface, I feel something. There is another hand on the other side of the mirror trying to touch me. It is right there! It's left hand to my right hand.

Over time, I come to realize that the other hand is a woman's hand. It is smaller than mine and cannot reach as high. I start having fantasies of gallantly freeing the trapped maiden in the glass. She would be sensual and beautiful. She would be loving and carefree. Most of all, she would be happy. But then what? I am already in a loving, committed relationship. But still, I know I have to free this being.

My daily meditations became clogged with scenarios of freeing my beautiful mystery woman. Any attempts to clear the images in my mind fail. Deciding I'm trying too hard, I let go. I remember lessons from my childhood religious training. "If you have the faith of a mustard seed, you could move a mountain."

At that time, those lessons did not work for me. First of all, I did not know what a mustard seed was. Second, how could one measure the amount of a belief or of a faith with the physical dimensions of a seed? Since then, I have learned to meditate and have built a faith, or better yet, a belief that I can create my reality. I admit that sometimes it works and sometimes it doesn't. I am still learning and have not yet tried to move a mountain.

Today, again, I stand at the mirror. I reach out and place my right hand on the surface, as I have done many times before. As I step back, I see the reflection of myself, full body with my arm stretched out. It is as if the image is flowing out from the mirror, through my hand and up my arm to reveal my whole body.

"Who are you?" I ask.

"I am you, or at least a part of you," I hear a voice say. "But I am missing in your reflection. I am in the mirror in another dimension, waiting to merge with you. That way, I can be a part of the image of you reflected in the mirror and also what is visible to other people."

Without thinking, or doubting, I reach down and lift the edge of the mirror. It's heavy, but not too heavy. I tell myself, "Don't make this too hard." I lift the bottom edge up on my knee, then up on my shoulder. It feels like a heavy drape, with the weight and bulk of stage curtains in a theater. I adjust my stance. Now it feels like I am shouldering a roll of carpet. For a moment, I am excited, distracted by my ability to lift this mirror. I look down. A beautiful female figure is wiggling out from under the mirror! She stands up, smiles at me, and steps towards me. When I drop the edge of the mirror, it rings like a bell or chimes. I open my arms, thinking she is going to embrace me, but she slips into me.

Merges with me!

I look at myself in the mirror.

I am smiling!

BEACH

Joseph rolls over, wakes up, or maybe he had not even been asleep. His mind is filled with what happened last night. He slides out of bed, careful not to waken Barbara, quickly dresses, grabs a jacket, and opens the sliding door just enough to slip out. It is first light, Joseph's favorite time of day.

Their room is on the ground floor of the motel, in the back facing the beach. It's just light enough for him to make his way down to the water. A gentle, onshore breeze brings in the clean, fresh smell of Monterey Bay. Joseph breathes in deeply, trying to clear his mind. Just above high tide line lays a storm-polished, driftwood log. It seems to shine brighter than the beach sand in the early morning light. Joseph sits on it and tries to center himself for meditation.

He learned to meditate a few months earlier, but no matter how many breathing techniques he tries, the monkey chatter in his brain will not stop. Last night's image of the blue light floating just above them, and his corresponding thoughts woven into their love making, keep churning in his mind.

They are both pushing forty. As the passion and intensity of their lovemaking increased over the past few months, Joseph realized that he had a great desire to conceive a child. But Barbara said no. She already had enough kids and didn't want another.

Joseph was carrying a little knot of emptiness deep in his gut. Day by day, the knot had stayed quiet. Sometimes, out of nowhere, the emotions seem to surround and engulf him. The knot was too large; he became the knot.

Maybe that's what the blue light last night was all about? As Joseph sits on the log, another idea comes to mind: the blue light was a spirit entity waiting, wanting to join in the conception of a child. A deep, gut-wrenching sob swells up out of the pain in his heart. Joseph buries his face in his hands.

"Oh," he cries. "My son, my son."

The first rays of sunlight warm Joseph's back. The breeze picks up. Opening his eyes, he sees the bay is filled with small white waves, shining bright, catching the low morning sunlight. He closes his eyes again. He feels calm. The warmth helps, and even though he doesn't want to admit it, the cry was even more helpful.

In his mind's eye, a small ship appears sailing into the bay. As it comes closer, Joseph can just make out that it's a 1700s Spanish vessel, a captivating design with blunt bow, high bowsprit, and a ridiculous tall stern castle. He plays with the image for a while, the white sails bright in the morning sun, then opens his eyes.

There, less than a quarter mile away, is the ship! A cold shiver flashes through his body. Joseph closes his eyes. The ship is there. Opening his eyes, the ship continues sailing towards him and the beach. Close, open, close again...the same ship.

The anchor is set, and a party of men row ashore. The crew hauls out barrels to fill with fresh water from a nearby stream. A young officer, dressed in a short blue jacket with brass buttons, walks up the beach and sits on the log next to Joseph. The man's thoughts and feelings radiate out with so much power, Joseph can hear them. He is all too familiar with this way of thinking, over and over again, playing out the memories and even more strongly the accompanying pain.

The story unfolds. José, the name of the young officer, was in love with a woman, and she with him. Her father disapproved of the romance. José came from a long line of skilled craftsmen, while the father was wealthy from his mercantile connections with the royal family. Even though José lived a comfortable life, he was no match to the father's expectations.

"What was her name?" asks Joseph.

"Barbara Maria."

The couple found ways to meet. José would climb up the ivy at the back of the house, below Barbara Maria's window. They spent many nights together, loving and laughing and talking about life. One night, after lovemaking, Barbara Maria said through her tears that this was to be the last night together. She was carrying José's child, and her father had found out. He would not allow her to marry her lover. Instead, she was to be sent to a convent, and the child in her was to be destroyed.

At this point in his story, the young officer begins to cry, sobbing, despite trying to hold back his tears. Joseph reaches out and puts his arm around the weeping man. "What happened next?"

"There was a knock, no, more like a banging, on the door." José answers. "I climbed down the ivy and ran as fast as I could to the port. Heard horses behind me and men shouting, looking for me."

As José relives his memories, Joseph sees the images as they unfold. José runs to a ship on which his family recently created beautiful woodwork in the captain's cabin. He is given a position as a junior officer. They sail the next day. José has not even asked where they were bound but is happy to learn the journey is up the coast of Mexico, maybe as far north as the city of Saint Francis.

"Hey, there you are," says Barbara, walking down from the motel. "It's so beautiful here. The waves in the bright sunshine look like little sailboats, and the bay—"

"Yes, it's like one can see forever," says Joseph. "I was just thinking…"

"Me too," says Barbara, "It was so wonderful last night. Let's see if we can get a late check out, grab a quick bite, and do it again."

"Sounds good to me," says Joseph, putting his arms around her and smiling as they embrace.

Later, while they are snuggling together, their thoughts drifting in and out, Joseph breaks the silence.

"Have you ever?" asks Joseph, raising up on one elbow, "have you ever thought of yourself as being Spanish?"

"You mean like in a past life?" asks Barbara.

"Yeah."

"Ha, I come from a long line of Hungarian Jews," says Barbara. "Not likely. Why?"

"Last night I had a dream," Joseph says. "We were together in Spain, and…"

"Oh, my God!" says Barbara, sitting up in bed. "I dreamt I was pregnant. I may have been in Spain, maybe, it smelled like Spain, whatever that is…everything was going so fast…"

"Did you have the child?" asks Joseph, "Did you give birth?"

Barbara slumps over and starts to cry. Joseph holds her.

"No, the nuns—" she sobs. "I lost the baby… Oh, God…"

Barbara picks up a tissue and blows her nose.

"I woke up, you were gone," she says. "The baby was gone… oh, I miss that child. In the past I have longed for him, but then I had my own kids, and kinda forgot until now."

"I had a dream early this morning too," says Joseph. "It involved Spain and a possible child. I feel a loss of that… of my son."

Barbara gives Joseph a loving hug. He faces her.

"Would you like to have a child together?"

"Oh, no," says Barbara. "I already have a family. I'm just about mothered out."

"Yeah, I can understand."

Joseph gets up, starts to put on his clothes, and turns away from Barbara so she will not see the grief, the pain in his heart, and the longing in his face.

Joseph takes a deep breath and thinks, Maybe in the next life.

The path along the bluff, for over thirty years, has been one of Joseph's go-to walks. He has stopped asking himself why he is so drawn to this place after all these years. He just is. The fresh ocean air, the view all the way out to the Farallon Islands, makes him feel like he's the lookout, high in the rigging of an old sailing ship. The feeling is as vivid as a memory. However, when the path meanders close to the edge of the bluff, above waves crashing on jagged rocks, Joseph senses a panic attack building in his chest. Even his legs start to wobble. Joseph relaxes when the path takes him away from the edge. That's why he likes to sit on the trunk of a coastal cypress, blown down in a storm long ago. He can see the ocean, but not the rocks and the crashing waves below the edge of the bluff.

Today, the sun is shining, but farther south near the Golden Gate Bridge the fog has rolled in. Joseph watches a man emerging from the mist, wearing a tattered blue jacket with brass buttons. The fog's dark damp edge clings to him. He is surprised to see Joseph.

"Have you seen it?" the man asks.

"Seen what?"

"The debris, the… the shipwreck," answers the man, "Have you seen any survivors? There must be some."

"No, nor any shipwreck, either."

"But you must have!" says the man, "It happened just last night, I think. Am I the only one? We were trying to make it into the city of Saint Francis. There was a strong onshore wind, but…"

"Here, sit," says Joseph, "And tell me what happened."

The man joins him on the cypress log. He studies Joseph for a few minutes. Looking out to the ocean, the man relates that yesterday, he, being young and with good eyesight, went aloft in the rigging to lookout for the shore. It was impossible to see through the fog. Suddenly, they were right on jagged shoreline. He called out a warning, but it was too late. The ship slammed against the rocks knocking him off the tall mast into the churning waves. He was crushed between the sinking ship and the rocky shore. When he awoke, he found himself wandering along the bluff, between darkness and light. He knew he was seriously injured. Blood dripped from wounds on his chest and legs, but he kept walking.

"I don't mean to intrude," says Joseph, staring at the blood-soaked hole in the man's jacket, "But I think walking between the dark and the light indicates that you're dead. You haven't let go and finished crossing over into your next life."

"Could be. If so, if I really died in the shipwreck, I don't know how to move on. The priest never told us."

"Neither do I," says Joseph. "But I think one just has to accept that it's okay to cross over."

"You look familiar…but your beard and hair are white," says the man. "And you're walking with a cane. Did I talk with you a few weeks ago when I went ashore with my crew to fill our water casks?"

"Perhaps," says Joseph. "Are you José?"

"Yes," says José. "We were sitting on a log and—"

"Talking about you and Barbara Maria and a possible child…" says Joseph.

"You had just seen a child, or its spirit that wanted to be born," says José.

"You're right," says Joseph. "But that was more than thirty years ago. And I think you and I are living three hundred years apart."

"That's hard to understand," says José.

"Yeah, but we are connected somehow with or through Barbara Maria."

"Well…" says José.

"Ah, but I have good news," says Joseph.

"What?"

"Barbara and I are married. Been so for more than twenty-five years."

"Do you think it's possible that you are me, and that I am you?" asks José. "I've never heard of that."

"Who knows?"

The men sit side by side for a while, thinking, trying to make sense of all this.

"Did you? Did I ever have the child with Barbara Maria? Was our son ever born?" asks José.

"No," says Joseph, "And I feel a deep sadness, a vast hollowness, and a great longing. I have felt this for my whole life. But even so, life is good with Barbara." Joseph laughs. "At least I no longer have to climb up the ivy on the back of her house to visit."

"Yes," says José. "That was tough. I had to be so quiet."

"It's too complex to figure this all out," says Joseph. "I guess we, you and I and whoever else we are, will just have to wait for the right time, in the right life, for our son to be born."

José stands and waves goodbye. He begins to fade into the dark fog.

"No, wait!" shouts Joseph. "Go into the light, not the dark."

He reaches out a hand to help José progress into the light.

The outstretched hand does not make contact. Joseph watches as the figure merges into a shimmering bright disk of light. It is so intense, he squeezes his eyes shut for just a moment. The sun behind warms his back. Joseph opens his eyes. The figure and the disk are no longer there, replaced by a long view up the coast to the north.

ANNABELLE AND *ANNIE TOO*

The fog is in. He stands on the boat deck, takes a deep breath welcoming the new day, and looks out to San Francisco Bay. The fog today is thick, heavy, and low, confined to the Golden Gate passage through the bluffs of the Headlands. The dense whiteness is compressed, focused, rolling forward with turbulence on its rush into the open waters of the Bay.

To the west, out in the ocean, the fog is impenetrable, crammed into the Bay through the narrow Golden Gate. The morning sun makes the fog shine with a whiteness and brightness that hurt his eyes. A ship is coming in through the Gate on the flood tide. Only the tops of its tall masts show above the fog. The ship's foghorn sends forward its warning. The sound carries a hint of apprehension. He wishes he could let the ship's captain know that out ahead in the open waters of the Bay, the leading edge of the fog is dissolving. It seems that particles of morning sunlight are fighting back the particles of fog, even as it rolls in from the ocean. It will not be long before the advancing fog is stopped. The fog bank will remain just offshore.

"Today will be a good day to sail," he says with a smile.

"He" is Capt'n Jack, aboard his 60-foot scow

schooner *Annie* in the late 1890s, anchored off the Sausalito waterfront.

"He" is twenty-eight-year-old David, aboard his 30-foot sloop *Annie Too* in the late 1990s, moored in the Sausalito Yacht Harbor.

David

It is a good time to be alive, late 1990s, and San Francisco is growing. Early June on San Francisco Bay. The wind is about five knots, the summer fog is burning off, and the tide through Raccoon Straights is timed for a great sail around Angel Island. Another perfect day.

Whoa! Why am I heading into Tiburon Harbor? I must have been daydreaming. Might as well stop for a hamburger and fries at Sam's, if there's room at the dock.

David likes to sail into Sam's dock (a bit of a show-off maneuver), bringing his 30-foot sailboat *Annie Too* into the turning basin and tying up at the small dock below the restaurant's deck.

Annie

Annie is sitting on the deck at Sam's—again. She's annoyed at herself for this juvenile behavior. Today she had wanted to go for a hike on Mt. Tam, continuing her exploration of the Bay Area, but instead had found herself turning towards Tiburon. This was the fourth, okay, fifth time she had returned in the past few weeks after seeing that guy in the sailboat. How many hamburgers could a girl eat?

But here she is again, hoping to see that guy.

She toyed with her fries, recalling the nightmarish round-trip ferry ride to Angel Island across Raccoon Strait. The little ferry was rolling around, and Annie at first thought she was seasick, but then she kept having the daydream of falling into darkness. Moving to the inside cabin helped a little, but whenever she closed her eyes, there was that same bad dream. She had gone into Sam's for something to eat after the ferry ride, and there was that tall guy with curly hair in his boat. When he looked up at her, the darkness of that bad dream that she was still carrying vanished with a flash, and she was surrounded in a bright glow. It was too much, and she panicked, ran out of the restaurant to her car. As soon as she moved her car she wanted to return but got caught in traffic and one-way streets. By the time she got back to the restaurant, the guy and his boat were gone.

Now, she is about to call the waitress and cancel her order when she notices him sailing up the channel. Her heart does a flip-flop, filling her with a warm glow.

David

A power boat is just leaving, the happy boaters not paying much attention to a sailboat sharing the same waterway, crowding David to the right side of the narrow channel and causing him to lose the wind. A quick tack, and the boat is back on course, but the forward momentum David had expected to use to maneuver to the dock is lost. This is, of course, part of the fun and the challenge of bringing a boat of this size into such a small moorage. David stands in the cockpit steering, his senses acutely aware of the microcosm around him: the wind speed and direction, the tide current around the dock, the other boats, what space there is in the turning basin, the small space at the dock. He is wondering if he can pick up enough speed to make the turn. He could always start the engine, but as a sailor that option is left for the escape clause. Some of the people on Sam's deck are watching the mini drama, but most are oblivious. For David, the people are not a part of the information input he is receiving to use in the maneuver which he must make in the next few seconds.

The channel has narrowed.

Glancing up, he sees her. The same golden-haired woman he saw a few weeks ago when he was making a similar approach to Sam's. Her eyes draw him into her gaze and send back a drawn-out flash of blue-white light. David locks into that light. All the senses that he had concentrated on his immediate surroundings are now focused within that beam. She smiles. Suddenly her eyebrows raise, and her mouth opens as if to speak. She breaks contact to look at something a few feet in front of him. David follows her gaze. He is bearing down on a boat tied at the end of the dock. He spins the wheel to port just as the wind makes a fluky gust around the roof of the restaurant, catching the sail and slamming it to the other side. David ducks as the boom swings over on a hard gybe. He misses the small boat but is now crosswise in the narrow channel with little forward motion for steering and no dependable wind. David keeps the boat turning as if to leave. Time to exit this embarrassing failed maneuver. Escape option:

Start the engine, run forward and lower the sails, run back and shift the transmission—wait, not into forward, but into reverse. David thought, *Why did I do that? Didn't know I was that dyslexic.* The boat slows, then stops and slowly begins backing. The wind picks up and blows against the mound of loose sails, pushing the boat sideways. By controlling the throttle and the rudder and using the wind, David slides the boat sideways into the dock space left by the power boat.

Annie

She figured this was just some kind of fantasy obsession. Then, there he was, parking his boat just below her table. When he looked up at her, it was just too much of a shock.

Capt'n Jack and the Scow Schooner

Captain Jack loved his ugly scow schooner: flat shovel bow, boxy hull, and flat stern. It was a good time to be alive, late 1890s, and San Francisco was growing faster than anyone had expected. Seemed that there were more horses than people and they all had to eat. The hay grew way up in Petaluma and all along the Sacramento River. The people in Petaluma and upriver needed things from the City, so this kept a fleet of about 400 scow schooners busy sailing the bay.

As with other scows, *Annie* was rigged as a schooner with a large main sail aft and a smaller fore sail forward. In addition, the schooner carried one or more head sails set on a bow sprit. Some scows even carried top sails, set between the top gaff and a top mast extension on the main mast. In all, the scow schooners carried a tremendous amount of sail area, which of course, was needed to handle the fifty to seventy tons of cargo. With their wide beam, and when empty without cargo, the scows were very fast!

Annie was not designed as a liveaboard. The space below deck was only about five feet high, just enough for seated head room. But with a stove and a few comforts, it became home for Jack while he finished the joinery work of the cabinets, bunks, and storage areas with wood from the lumber mill in nearby Mill Valley. He built a "pilot house" cabin at the stern, even though this would reduce the deck area for carrying cargo. It gave Jack a more comfortable living space and a refuge from the weather, with cold fog so common to San Francisco. Another ingenious addition was the extension of the wheel steering up to the roof of the cabin. This allowed the helmsman to see over the cargo stacked high on the deck. By Spring, Jack and *Annie* were ready for work. After a shakedown cruise around Angel Island, Jack picked up a load of redwood siding from the Mill Valley Lumber Company for delivery to Napa. The lumber was loaded athwartship, which made it easier to load on and off when the boat was tied alongside the shore. So began a life of work and sailing.

Life On the Water

Jack, or Capt'n Jack as he like to be called, had a good head for business. He would often pick up the tail end of a load of cargo, which had been too much for one scow, knowing that with a lighter load and his fast boat, he could overtake and arrive at the destination sooner than the more heavily laden boat. Jack could negotiate a price for his load and the larger one that would follow a few hours behind. The other captains liked this arrangement because they did not like the process of "negotiating" a price for cargo, and Jack made a small percentage of the deal. Before long, Jack had a large group of business friends around the bay, and he was rarely without a hauling contract. Hay from Petaluma and sacks of wheat from Sacramento to San Francisco. Bricks from Larkspur, and lumber from Mill Valley to everywhere buildings were going up, which seemed like everywhere.

If work was slow, there were always oyster shells in the South Bay. The scow would be anchored over the beds, with the tide out, and with the boat resting on the mud, the shells could be loaded on board. It was heavy, dirty work, but the shells were free for the taking. With the next high tide, the scow would float off and the shells delivered to Petaluma to be ground for chicken feed. Loading sand from the Napa River at low tide was another "free" enterprise.

But the business Jack liked best was the buying and selling of his own cargo. He had the cash, sometimes as much as $5,000, to purchase a load of lumber or hay or whatever, and then find a buyer somewhere in the Bay. The Bay was not the only market area. Some of Jack's friends sailed their scow schooners out the Golden Gate and up the coast to Bolinas and even farther North into Tomales Bay to reach Point Reyes and Paper Mill Creek at the South end of Tomales Bay. But Jack knew the dangers of crossing the bar at Tomales Bay: ever-shifting sand bars, turbulent surf created by the outgoing tide and strong onshore winds. What's more, he enjoyed sailing in San Francisco Bay. The trip to Sacramento was always a money maker, so much material was needed there and on up into the gold country. But it was a three-day run from San Francisco to Sacramento, which meant two nights tied up in the river. The mosquitoes were so bad in the Sacramento River delta that sleep was almost impossible. A smoky kerosene lamp was kept burning in the cabin, but even so, the mosquitoes usually won. And if the wind and tides were not right, the trip could take sixteen days!

Jack's most enjoyable route was the San Francisco to Napa run. Jack always felt lighthearted leaving the Napa River with a load of fruits, vegetables, and nuts bound for San Francisco. He was a farm boy at heart and loved the smell of fresh produce. And, as he said, he would never go hungry on the way to San Francisco. If the tide and wind were right, the trip could be made in a day. However, sometimes the tide would change, or the wind would die before he made it up to Napa. Then Jack had to decide whether to tie to the shore, and wait for the tide change, or to kedge his way upriver. Sometimes, when tied to the shore, a farmer would see his masts rising above the riverbank and would bring a wagon or two of produce or firewood to sell to Jack. A wagon load was nowhere near the fifty to seventy tons the *Annie* could carry, but it made for good business. Jack tried to avoid kedging. It meant rowing the small boat, loaded with the anchor and a long line, a few hundred feet upriver, setting the anchor, and then pulling in the line with the windless on *Annie's* bow. Meanwhile, the other anchor was being rowed upriver to be set. It was hard work, took three men, but the schooner did move upriver slowly, one anchor set after another.

He loved pushing the limits of his boat. Sometime, if the wind and tide were blowing and flowing to his advantage, Jack would sail through Raccoon Straights on the ebb tide, out into the open Bay to catch the tide change. Riding the flood tide and strong on shore wind, *Annie* sped into the San Francisco waterfront and to home.

Lars

It was on one such a maneuver that a man was seen struggling in the tide rip in the open bay. Jack gave the order to come about and set a tack to the floundering man. The scow schooner was a "handy" boat with its flat bottom without a long keel, but with a deep center board and large rudder, it was easily tacked even in the cross currents of the rip tide. Jack tacked *Annie* up wind, stopping the forward motion, and allowed the boat to drift downwind to the rescue. The man was very large and almost dead.

"Ahoy there, can you catch this line?"

Jack threw a line with a bowline already tied at the end.

"He's too weak to even slip into the bight. You there!" Jack said to one of his crew, "jump in!" The crewman swam to the man and slipped the line over his chest and under his arms.

It took Jack and his crew a good twenty minutes to pull him up into the boat, even using the boom of the foremast as a derrick. The exhausted man tried to be of help but was so weak he could not even stand. Jack put him below deck on a bunk near the warm stove and fed him supper of beans, onions, and dried beef. After only a few bites of food, the man fell into a deep sleep. The next day the man was awake but was not responsive to Jack's questions. Jack had learned some Norwegian from other sailors while sailing on the high seas, and upon hearing these words, the man spoke. His name was Lars. He had jumped overboard from a freighter, his clothes and papers wrapped in an oil skin. He lost the floating packet, and with the current stronger and colder than he had expected, he almost perished.

Lars became Jack's steady crew. Other crew came and went by their own choice or by the amount of work to be had. But Lars stayed on, never talking much, but a steady and powerful worker. Jack paid him the going rate of forty dollars per month, which was more than the wages of a blue water sailor. Lars often seemed to be embarrassed to take the money. Many months later, Jack asked:

"Lars, what are you thinking about as you so often stand at the bow, staring out at the water?"

Lars replied, "I am remembering the day of my rescue. I was sure that I had died. I could see angels hovering over me. I could also see dark shapes in the depths below that seemed to be calling to me to let go and sink down to them. As the *Annie* sailed in close, I thought the white sails were the wings of a large angel coming to take me to heaven. I'm now content to be in the safety of *Annie*."

Lars took over much of the daily work of running the scow schooner, even making some of the hauls himself. This freed Capt'n Jack to contract for more work, to buy a house near the channel, get married, and have a child. All in the space of a year and a half. Mary was the daughter of one of the other scow captains, a man Jack had worked with and had become friends with in his early days in San Francisco. Jack had known Mary for some time and was attracted to her fiery temperament, and to be honest, to her fiery passion. They had a daughter not long after they were married; no one seemed to be bothered counting the months. Their daughter had her mother's blue eyes and reddish hair.

"I think we should call our daughter Annie," said Jack, smiling. "After all, she has a boat named after her."

"No," Mary replied, "if you like the name Annie, then we will call her Annabelle."

Annabelle

Laying on top of the load of hay, Annabelle stares up at the full, white canvas. The sails are pulling taut in the wind. The surface moves, like the breasts of a woman breathing. The rolling of the scow schooner has once again lulled her into a daydream. It is always the same dream, with only small changes; the gentle rolling of the boat and the curve of the sails above her transports Annabelle back in the arms of her mother, held close to the curve of her breasts. Looking up, she can see her mother's face. Eyes the color of the summer sky, framed with bright golden red hair. It has been five years since her mother died, but she still misses her. Father's new wife, Mother Susan, is very nice, but it is not the same. Now that there is a new baby boy, Annabelle wonders if she is losing her father's love. When she shyly mentioned it, her father held her and told her that there was plenty of love to go around. "Love goes on forever and ever."

They had become very close after her mother's death. With no one else in the family, Father had taken little seven-year-old Annabelle with him on hay runs. She had become a good sailor, handling the sails, cleating mooring lines, and even taking the helm and steering a course across the Bay. She wore work clothes, mostly bib overalls, like the other men and boys on the docks. Her hair was tucked up under a cap, so crews on other boats thought she was a boy. She almost never wore shoes, her bare feet toughened by the wood deck and the ropes she used to climb the masts. Often, after the cargo had been unloaded, there would be an impromptu race between the scow schooner's crews as to who could climb a mast the fastest; Annabelle often won!

In the long evenings, anchored somewhere in the vast waterways of the San Francisco Bay, waiting for first light to continue their haul, Capt'n Jack and Annie would sit at their small table and share the light of a single kerosene lantern. Jack had taught Annie to read and to do her numbers. She was a quick learner with an inexhaustible supply of questions. His stories of sailing the seas, along with a world map, gave her a good knowledge of what was beyond San Francisco. Annie learned to write by copying out long passages written by notable authors such as Walt Whitman, Emily Dickinson, and her favorite, Mark Twain. She enjoyed his humor and insight into the world around him. She had tried reading Herman Melville but found him too dark and too wordy. Her father, on the other hand, enjoyed reading aloud passages of Melville with his description of the sea and the life of a sailor. Often, after reading from

Melville, Jack would sit for a few minutes deep in thought. Looking up, he would say, "I am so thankful that I am no longer a deep-water sailor."

"Me, too," was her reply.

As Annabelle lies on top of the hay bales, looking up at the curved breast-like sails, she slips her hand inside her shirt and feels the small buds of her own breasts. The snaps on her bib overalls are making them sore, and she knows that soon she will have to stop wearing boy's clothes. Mother Susan is making a new dress for her, and hoping that Annabelle will learn to sew, has encouraged her to work on it. It is light blue like her mother's eyes, and has many, many layers of petticoats. Annabelle is looking forward to wearing the dress but is also afraid that once she puts it on, she will never wear boy's clothes again. Susan has been telling her about becoming a woman, which is okay. Annabelle likes taking care of baby John, but she prefers sailing and being with Father. She knows that other girls stay at home and help their mothers. But her father needs her, at least until baby John grows up. Thinking about not being on the boat with her father any more makes her heart heavy and her stomach ache, even worse than when she overhears Father and Mother Susan arguing about her.

"It is time for her to stay home and learn the 'womanly' arts of cooking, housekeeping, sewing, and baby care," Mother Susan would argue.

"Yes, yes, I know, but there's plenty of time for all that," said Jack. "For now, I need Annabelle as a crew member on the boat. I can't do my work without her help. Why, the way things are going, she may be the first woman scow captain on San Francisco Bay."

"But she is first of all a woman," Mother Susan replied.

"Annabelle, Annabelle where are you?"

Uh, oh, thought Annabelle. Father must have been calling for a long time, because he usually calls me 'Annie'.

"Yes, Father?"

"Hurry, the tide is changing. Come down and take the helm, while I set the anchor. In the morning, we'll catch the ebb tide at first light. If there's wind in the morning, we should be able to make San Francisco before the flood tide. Also, I have surprise for you— a book of poems. And Mother Susan has sent a gift for you as well."

In the Beginning

David tried not to stumble as he tied up his boat to Sam's dock. She was sitting at a table just above him, just like the time before, staring right at him with those pixie eyes. *God, I hope she doesn't leave.* David cleated the bow line and stern line. He was careful to tie his lines under the other boat's mooring lines. This way, if the other boats left before him, his lines would not have to be re-tied. Because the space was so short, David added two spring lines to keep his boat from drifting too far forward or back. He glanced up. She was still there, and he thought she was watching him. David realized that he was feeling a combination of a chill, a sweat, weak knees, dry mouth, and his heart fluttering.

The hostess at the top of the ramp said that there was a twenty-to-thirty-minute wait for a deck table. David replied that he was meeting a friend. The hostess looked skeptical, but when he gestured to the woman, she was beaming at him. *God, what a smile!* David walked towards her and she placed her left elbow over the back of her chair, still smiling. This movement tightened the light cotton fabric of her blouse over her left breast with just the faint hint of the nipple pressing through. David admonished himself, *Don't stare at her breast! Don't stare at her breast. It's not cool, don't stare at her breast.* He was trying to think of what to say. He had heard that a woman is impressed or turned off within the first thirty seconds of a meeting. But all he could think was, *Don't stare at her breast.*

"May I share your table?" he asked. "There's a thirty minute wait and... uh, or are you expecting—?"

"Yes, sit down, and I am not pregnant."

David collapsed into the chair, his mind both racing and drawing a blank, all the successful lines he had thought of in the past gone.

"I didn't mean, ah..."

"I know, I just couldn't help myself, it was a perfect, well, you know."

David, unable to think what to say, just blurted out, "I've seen you before. Here..."

Annie smiled. She liked this line. Most guys would say, "Haven't I seen you before?" which would require a response. And whatever it was, the response put the girl in the defensive.

"Yes, a few weeks ago."

"But when I came up on the deck, you were gone, and..."

"Yeah, I had to leave." Annie wanted to say she was sorry, she had panicked, and that when she returned, he was gone. But she didn't. She just looked down at the table, not knowing how to explain the dark gloom hovering at the periphery of her consciousness.

"Well, I'm glad you're here now."

Again, no questions, just a statement about the present. Annie felt a flutter in her heart. The darkness retreated.

The waitress came with Annie's order and asked David what he wanted.

Annie touched his arm. "Why don't we share my burger? It's more than I want, and you can order something else."

"Oh good, I'll have a Caesar salad and an iced tea."

They ate in silence, each trying to think of something to say. Annie began, "I like your boat."

"Thanks"

"I don't like your boat... I mean I like your boat okay, but what I really like is the name *Annie Too*.

"How come?"

"My name is Annie, too."

"Wow! A great name for a boat, if I do say so myself, but who would have named a child *Annie Too?*"

"Noooooooooo"

"Well..." David grinned. "I guess that's a better name then *I'M PREGNANT TOO*"

"Touché!"

Annie studied the boat for a while. "Why does it say 'Sausalito' under the name?"

"That is where I keep her. It's a great moorage. I can walk up the dock to the street to a good coffee house and I'm just a block or so from the shops."

"Why is there that little sail on the back of the boat, it doesn't look the same as the other bigger sail?"

"It's called a spanker, and..."

"Spank her! Sounds kinky to me!"

"Well, in a way. The old square rigged sailing ships had a spanker. That sail helps to turn the boat more quickly, kind of giving her a spanking to push her around the turn. You see, if ... wait a minute. This is too much technical stuff. I like to putter around the boat and try different ideas and designs. That sail has a 'snotter'..."

Annie held her napkin to her face to cover her laugh. "A what? Did I hear you say—»

"Yes, a snotter. It's a small line or rope that attaches—»

"Are you one of those guys that's suffering from arrested development? I have a nephew in the sixth grade, and he loves to use words about body functions, and then he giggles."

"Hmm, maybe, it is fun to throw that word around in a conversation."

Annie nodded, smiling. "At least you're honest, and you don't giggle, you kept a straight face. Now I know about your boat, where it lives."

"Moored."

"Ok, moored, and that you are honest about—"

"I never tell a lie."

"What I'm trying to say is that I don't know your name."

"Oh, I'm sorry, my name is David, and..."

Annie sucked in a shaky breath and shook her head in denial. Seeming to regain her cool, she quipped, "Oh, the killer of giants and seducer of other men's wives."

"Yea, but he was a good king, too. And he appreciated a beautiful woman. Just look around the deck. There are a number of women sitting alone at tables, and I picked you to sit with."

"Yeah, yeah. It's starting to get deep in here. Look, I have three older brothers and I know how guys think. It was my smile that brought you to my table, wasn't it?"

"That's exactly what I was saying, your smile is a part of your beauty. And, by the way, I have an older sister, so I too know some things. Anyway, I prefer to think of 'David' the way Michelangelo sculpted him. Are you familiar with the sculpture?"

With these words, David turned to show his profile, assuming an exaggerated regal pose.

Annie's eyes widened, but she hid her reaction by drinking water. By the time he turned back, Annie had recovered. "Yes, I am. Very," she said. "Well, there is the curly hair, the chin is not the same, yeah, big hands, and we all know what that means, but you are not ten-feet tall, and I can't tell if you're circumcised or not."

David just shook his head, not knowing how to respond.

"I'm sorry, I should not have said that. I know you guys are sensitive about those things. But after all, isn't that the first thing everyone looks at when they see the sculpture?"

"No, no, that's okay, I may not be ten-feet tall, ah…umm, I do look a lot like, well, you know…"

"Right," Annie said, blushing.

They turned their attention back to eating the burger.

"How did your boat come to have the name *Annie Too*?"

"When I was nine years old, my dad was given a boat by a friend. It was just a little day sailor, and its name was *Annie Too*. My dad and I had some wonderful times together learning to sail, made lots of mistakes, but it was really great! We had a lot of fun together."

David noticed a shadow of sadness pass over Annie's face, but then her smile returned.

"Have you ever sailed?" David asked.

"No, I want to, but I think I'm a little scared to. You know, we don't have a lot of water in Kansas."

"Oh, you're from Kansas? I thought you were a city girl."

"Why?"

"Because of your quick uptake."

"Oh, I know. It drives my family nuts. They think I'm interrupting all the time." Annie paused. "But I did live in New York City for a while, just before I went to Italy, and then I came to San Francisco, about eight months ago."

David leans forward and says, with an intensity he had not intended, "Tell me more about yourself."

"I was raised on a farm in western Kansas, near Dodge City."

"Yee-haw! Wyatt Earp and six shooters blazing!"

"Now that's interrupting, not New York up take."

"Sorry."

"Like I said, we raised wheat and cattle, and three older brothers."

"I thought one raised wheat and cattle, and children were..."

"Yep! Fetched up," Annie said in an exaggerated western drawl.

They both laughed. The waitress brought the salad and an extra plate.

"Ah, um, you go first."

"No, you go first."

"I've been doing all the talking."

"Oh no, most guys after 45 minutes would say, 'Enough about me, now let me tell you about my job.'"

"But I really want to know about you!"

"Okay, in a nutshell, like I said, I have three older brothers, all born in September or October, do the math: long winter nights on the cold prairie. I was a tag-a-long baby, born eight years after the youngest brother. I was born in March, which means I was conceived in mid-summer, the busiest time of the year on the farm. Sometimes, my dad would work around the clock during harvest, even sleeping in the truck out in the field for a few hours. Until my brothers got old enough to help, my dad hired harvest crews to help with the work. So, my dad never really thought I was his. He was never mean to me, just more or less ignored me."

Annie picked at her lunch. David wanted to reach out to take her hand but didn't. "How could your dad think that?"

"Well, both parents have brown eyes, and all my brothers have brown eyes, but my eyes are blue," said Annie, "and my hair is golden red, not brown." Annie looked up and David studied her eyes, thinking, *You have the most beautiful eyes I have ever seen. The blue is as light and clear as a summer sky, and with a ring of deep, dark blue around the outside.*

He broke the silence, "When I was sailing up the channel just now, there was a flash of blue-white light from your eyes, must have been the sunlight shining just—"

Annie reached over and touched his hand. "I felt it too! I thought it came from *your* eyes!"

Oh, No!

They held hands for a long time, just looking at each other. Suddenly, David felt a cold gust of wind and a growing darkness. A shiver went through him. The fog was coming in, bringing frigid wind and blotting out the last of the afternoon's sun. He looked back at Annie. She was gazing over his shoulder out to Raccoon Straits. Her face paled, and her chin quivered in fear and dread. David jumped up, thinking someone was behind them. In the distance, the gaff sail of the scow schooner *Alma* disappeared around the point. Why were they out in this nasty weather? It was going to be a rough, cold sail back to his berth in Sausalito. "I've got to go down and check the lines," he told Annie. "On my boat."

All the mooring lines were secure, but most of the other boats had left. He again felt a chill and wished he had ordered hot coffee, not iced tea. It was really getting dark out in the Straits. The fog was boiling in faster than he had ever seen. David raced back to the table to pay. Annie was gone! The waitress said she'd already paid the bill. *Damn!* he muttered, *I didn't even get her phone number or last name, damn, damn. Damn!* He ran out on Tiburon Boulevard looking and calling her name but saw only red tail-lights disappearing around the corner.

Annie gripped the steering wheel of her car, her mind racing. What is it about this place that attracts me, and at the same time has so much terrifying darkness around it?

She had felt the change in the weather, and shivering, looked up to see the black sail of that ugly boat silhouetted against the swirling grey fog. The shiver went clear to her heart and would not stop.

She had to get away. She felt as if she were suffocating.

She gulped deep breaths, heart pulsing in her ears. Driving away helped some. She was sorry, more sorry than called for, to leave David. She had heard him calling, but she had to get away. When he jumped up so quickly, it startled her, and then he seemed more interested in his boat than in the darkness rolling towards her.

Of course. He couldn't feel it.

She was alone with her terror.

The Poem

In the evening, after supper of rice and red beans, an easy clean up, and quick check of the anchor line, Capt'n Jack brings out his surprise and the gift from Mother Susan—a pair of shiny black patent leather shoes.

"Aren't they fine?" he says.

Annie had been hoping for drawing pencils, but she thanks her father.

"And now, the book of poems." Her father hands her a package wrapped in oil cloth. "I have not read it yet, but I liked the title."

They begin to read.

Annabel Lee
By Edgar Allan Poe, 1849

It was many and many a year ago,
In a kingdom by the sea,
That a maiden there lived whom you may know
By the name of Annabel Lee;
And this maiden she lived with no other thought
Than to love and be loved by me.

I was a child and she was a child,
In this kingdom by the sea,
But we loved with a love that was more than love—
I and my Annabel Lee—
With a love that the winged seraphs of Heaven
Coveted her and me.

And this was the reason that, long ago,
In this kingdom by the sea,
A wind blew out of a cloud, chilling
My beautiful Annabel Lee;
So that her highborn kinsmen came
And bore her away from me,
To shut her up in a sepulcher
In this kingdom by the sea.

The angels, not half so happy in Heaven,
Went envying her and me—
Yes!—that was the reason (as all men know,
In this kingdom by the sea)
That the wind came out of the cloud by night,
Chilling and killing my Annabel Lee.

Annie sees tears glistening on her father's
cheeks in the lantern's light. She had never
before seen her father cry.

But our love it was stronger by far than the love
Of those who were older than we—
Of many far wiser than we—
And neither the angels in Heaven above
Nor the demons down under the sea
Can ever dissever my soul from the soul
Of the beautiful Annabel Lee;

For the moon never beams, without bringing me dreams
Of the beautiful Annabel Lee;
And the stars never rise, but I feel the bright eyes
Of the beautiful Annabel Lee;
And so, all the night-tide, I lie down by the side
Of my darling—my darling—my life and my bride,
In her sepulcher there by the sea—
In her tomb by the sounding sea.

More tears stream down her father's face. He stands up and goes out on deck. Annabel follows and takes his hand. "Father," she says, "You see… It is not me… It was Annabel Lee."

He smiles at her attempt to comfort him. "I am not crying for Annabel Lee, but for the power of love," Jack says, "I have said to you, love can go on forever and ever."

"Are you ever worried or frightened about anything?" she asks.

"No, I think worrying is just saying a prayer for what you do not want. I believe that things will always work out."

Annabel smiles, remembering how things did seem to work out.

"However, I am aware of some things. Someday you will grow up and go your own way," Jack says.

"Maybe I will be the captain of my own scow," Annie says proudly.

After some thought, Jack adds, "Well maybe, but last week I saw a petrol engine in San Francisco that just might fit on one of the scow schooners."

"But you have always said that engines would not fit in a scow."

"Steam has never been practical," says Jack. "The boiler, engine and fuel storage just take up too much space and weight. You need a whole boat just to carry its own steam engine, but a petrol engine could work. Then the days of sail will be over. As much as I love this boat, I think I would sell her and buy a farm in the Napa Valley. I think Mother Susan would like that."

"I do not think I would like to be the captain of a motor-powered scow," says Annie, "Too much noise and stink. Anyway, I like sailing with you."

Jack embraces her. "Alas my child, change comes whether we welcome it or not. Off to your bunk now."

The Photographer

Capt'n Jack, and with him Annabelle, were often away from home for the weekend, but this was different. Susan had taken Annabelle shopping to buy new black patent leather shoes and "women's dainties," as she called them. Annabelle was surprised at how many layers of

scratchy petticoats she would have to wear under her new dress, along with bloomers. Sunday came and the garment was ready. The whole family dressed in their "Sunday Go To Meet'n" finery to go to church. Religion set lightly on Capt'n Jack. Church was a time for relaxing, meeting other people, and a break from the hard work of the week. After church, the family often went to the boat with a picnic basket filled with dinner.

When they arrived at the boat, Father said there was a surprise. He had hired a photographer to take pictures of his family on the boat. Annabelle had mixed feelings about the photographs being taken. She was happy that she was dressed in her new outfit, because it pleased her father and Mother Susan. But she also wished that there could be a photograph of just her father and herself, as it had been for a long time, with her dressed in bib overalls and cap.

The photographer set up his camera on the deck and the family lined up on the rail of the scow schooner, Annabelle on one side of Father and Mother Susan holding baby John on the other. Father had set the foresail as a background for the photograph. When the wind filled the sail, the boat tugged hard at the mooring lines, trying to sail free.

As soon as the photographer finished, Annabelle wanted to change back into her overalls, but Mother Susan forbade it, saying, "You're a lovely girl. There'll be trouble if you don't start dressing like a respectable young lady."

Hot, itchy, and constricted by tight lacing, Annabelle went forward to sulk by herself. The boat suddenly jerked against the restrictions of the mooring lines. Annabelle barely caught her balance in her slippery, leather-soled shoes. Much different from bare feet on the wooden deck. She pulled off the tight shoes. At least her feet could be free, for now.

The Ride Back

David was really pissed! Damn, damn, DAMN! Why had she run away like that? He was more mad at himself for not getting her phone number or at least her last name. He had to admit that his turning into Sam's dock earlier was, in honesty, the hope of seeing her again. And now she had run away. Maybe she had also run away before. Maybe she was unstable. Nope, there was something bothering her. She saw something that frightened her, but he hadn't seen it.

He had spent more time talking with her than he realized. The fog had rolled in with a vengeance, the wind was up, and the tide had changed. It was going to be a rough, wet ride back to Sausalito. In the mood he was in, David decided to motor back. Before he left the dock, he stowed the sails but left the mizzen sail up. It would help make the ride back smoother. Leaving Sam's dock and motoring out to Raccoon Straits, the wind was even stronger, and the waves had built up to where it was uncomfortable. David was glad he had remembered to set the mizzen, as it reduced the rolling motion. Twenty minutes into this wet, rough ride, David decided to stay on the boat that night rather than driving home. He lashed the wheel and went below to start the cabin heater which ran on the engine heat. At least it would be warm when he reached his moorage. When he returned to the cockpit, it seemed even colder. He thought again how nice it would be to have a pilot house with inside steering. David spent the rest of the trip trying not to think about Annie. But the more he thought of a pilot house cabin, the more he thought of spending nights in the pilot house with Annie.

The *Annie Too* turned into the mooring basin. The fog was thick and wet, but in the lee of the Sausalito hills there was much less wind. David released the snotter and shipped the sail's yard. He usually laid the yard against the mast and rolled up the sail, lashing it all together with the snotter, but tonight he left the small sail to gently flap. David slowed, and maneuvering with the engine at idle, slipped into his berth. As soon as the boat stopped, David switched on the spreader lights, tossed the mooring lines on the dock, and stepped off the boat. The soft glow of the lights lit the deck and a little of the dock next to the boat. David tied the stern line first and when he turned to go forward to tie the bow line, there was someone just in the edge of the light, tying the bow line.

"David?" came a small voice.

"Annie!"

David jumped, slipped on the wet dock, recovered, but was moving too fast to stop, and collided with Annie, taking her in his arms.

"I'm so sorry I ran away. I was so frightened, that dark..." Her voice trailed off.

"Well, you're here now. My God, you're so cold!" David ran his hands over her arms and down her back. "And wet, too. Let's get you aboard and dried off. Be careful, the dock and deck are wet and slippery."

"I already fell once," Annie said. "I'm a muddy mess."

David quickly plugged in the shore power cord and, checking the bow line, noticed that it had been cleated in a neat figure eight. David opened the hatch, and they went below into the cabin.

"Oh, it is so nice and warm in here."

David moved around the cramped cabin and found a towel and a dry outfit. "Get out of those wet things, dry off and put on the sweatsuit," he said. "Now that we have shore power, I'll put on the tea kettle. I'll have mint tea, but I have other teas, so help yourself. I'm going up to the rest room and will be back in a few minutes. The toilet's in there. It's called a 'head' on a boat. Just follow the directions to flush, makes an awful noise, but that's normal."

David turned to leave, then stopped. "Please don't run away again, but if you have to, leave me your phone number." He couldn't tell if she was laughing or crying as he left.

He had planned to take a shower but forgot to bring a towel. As he returned to the boat the sound of the head flushing signaled that Annie was not quite ready for his return.

David stopped and waited. He wondered if Annie would crawl into his sleeping bag, and if she would smell the last woman that had been there. He had been having a beer up at the bar, when a woman came over and started to talk. It was obvious that she was pretty horny. One thing led to another, and they ended up on his boat. And again one thing lead to another, and they were in his sleeping bag with no clothes. This woman had been wearing a lot of perfume, which was not a turn on for David. He lost his erection. Again, one thing led to another, and the evening was a disaster. He had not dated or been with a woman since but had found himself daydreaming about the woman on the dock at Sam's. And now she was actually in his cabin!

David stepped aboard. Annie was wrapped up in his sleeping bag, leaning back against the end of the bunk, holding a mug of tea. "Your tea is ready."

She had poured his tea and had placed a saucer over the top to keep it warm. The mug was placed on a shelf near the other end of the bunk. David sat down and leaned back, holding the warm mug, and faced Annie. The warmth felt good. He wished he could slip in under the sleeping bag too. They looked at each other for a minute or so. David felt Annie's foot pressing against his thigh. He slipped his hand under and touched her foot. "Wow! Your feet are cold."

He jumped up, found a one-liter water bottle, and filled it with hot water. Returning to the bunk, he put the bottle next to her bare feet. This gave him an excuse to touch her feet under the covers.

"That feels very nice. David, I need to tell you what happened this afternoon. It's a long story, but I must tell you."

"I'm here," he said.

"When I was a little girl, I used to have these awful dreams of sinking into darkness. I would call out 'Mommy, mommy' and sometimes a beautiful red headed woman would come to me. Other times, I would awaken being held by my mother against her chest with my head against her breast. Then as I grew up the dreams came less often, usually only when I was sad, like when things weren't going well in my relationship."

"What relationship?"

"Shhh... that is not a part of this story... well... not about this story at this time. Like I said this afternoon, I like to explore the Bay Area. I really loved the ferry rides between S.F. and Sausalito and other places. I took the ferry from Tiburon to Angel Island a few weeks ago and had an awful recurrence of that childhood dream, except this was a DAYDREAM! After the ferry ride I stopped to get something to eat, thinking that might help with the darkness that was seeming to follow me. Then I saw you sailing up the channel, and the darkness lifted and I was in a light, happy place. The darkness had never lifted like that before, and I guess I got 'cold feet' and ran away."

"You still have cold feet, but they're getting warmer."

"Yes, and you're helping in more ways than you know. Let me finish. I knew there was something special about you, and I returned to that restaurant numerous times, hoping to see you again. I sound like a crazy stalker."

David patted her arm. "No. Well, a little, but a really cute stalker. Please, continue. The jury is still out."

Annie nodded. "And then I saw you again today, standing up in your boat... and we looked at each other... and there was that flash of blue light... You seemed so focused on us."

"Yeah, I almost rammed that other boat. Thanks for the heads up."

"There's something else about the dream I haven't told you. Or anyone. In the dream, as I'm sinking into the darkness, I see a sailboat moving away. There's a man standing at the rail trying to reach out to me. There was such love and sadness in his eyes, trying, trying to make contact with me. Sometimes, when I think about the dream, feel that longing— his... mine... ours— and I cry for his sadness, and for mine."

There were tears in Annie's eyes, and David felt a tightness in his own throat.

"Then we had the talk today, and all was going so well, and there was the boat's name thing, your name David and sculpture of David."

"What about the sculpture?"

"I'll tell you later. Well, when the fog came in and it got darker, I looked out to the open water, and I saw that same boat that was in my dream, but the man was not standing at the rail like in the dream. When you jumped up and turned away, you seemed more interested in your boat than the bad dream I was in. I felt that I was not only losing that contact I had with you, but that I had lost the contact with the man on the boat. And even though that contact was very sad, there was also so much love there, too." She shook her head. "Too many feelings. After I left, I realized that you couldn't have seen the bad dream, only the startle in my eyes, and that you were naturally concerned about your boat in the changing weather." She sipped her tea. "I knew that the contact I had made with you was real and the dream was not, and I had to find you. I came to Sausalito, to the coffee shop you mentioned. So, I walked around the docks looking for you, getting soaked with fog, and all the boats look alike, but then I saw that kinky sail on the back of your boat, and I knew it was you." Annie looked down into her tea mug, seeming to be embarrassed for saying so much.

"And then you cleated the bow line with just the right amount of tension and with a beautiful figure eight tie. Most people don't know how to do a proper tie. They go around and around and up and over and up and over and around again. So where did you learn to do that tie?"

"I don't know, I have never been on a boat in my life, except for the ferry rides."

With this, both became silent.

Annie yawned. "Hey, did you put some kind of sleeping potion in my tea? I am so sleepy..."

"Me, too."

"Would you mind if I stayed here tonight? I don't think I could drive home."

Without waiting for an answer, Annie rolled over, leaving plenty of room for David in the narrow bunk.

David stood up, cleared the teacups, and straightened up the cabin. He hung up Annie's slacks and blouse to dry. Picking up her bra, he was tempted to look at the label, but realized, whatever size her breasts were, they seemed perfect to him. David did not dare take off his pants, knowing what would happen. After removing his keys, knife, wallet, and belt with his new cell phone hanging in its case, he turned out the cabin lights and slipped into the sleeping bag.

What's A Guy to Do?

Should he lay with his back to her or face her? That's a "no brainer." Now the age-old question of what to do with his arms; he could sleep on his left arm, but what to do with his right arm. He gently laid his arm on her waist. She pressed back against him. David had been aware that picking up her bra had started to give him an erection. He hoped that the activities of getting ready for bed would stop the erection, but now it was coming back with all urgency, and it was tangled up in his shorts demanding to be let free. David started to gently move his hand away from Annie's waist to straighten himself out, but she grabbed his hand with both of hers and pulled them to her chest. What's a guy to do? He cupped her breast and felt the firm nipple in the palm of his hand. Not only were they perfect, but holding her breast filled him with warmth and joy. David remembered the words of a gospel song he had heard years ago, "He has the whole world in His hands..." and wondered if "He" felt the same joy that he himself was feeling. David's erection was full on. She had to be able to feel it as she pressed against him. He wondered if she was inviting him to continue the seduction, but then he heard the soft, faint purr of a kitten, only much slower. Annie was asleep.

David wakened with a start. He knew he was on his boat, but something was different. Quickly, he realized that Annie was crawling over him.

"Shh, go back to sleep, I'm just going to pee."

David felt the boat rock as she stepped off. He thought, she did not take the restroom key. He heard a faint splash, like the sound of a bilge pump discharge. The boat rocked again and Annie came into the cabin.

"Off the dock?"

"Of course, you guys do."

"But...

"Look, my brothers and I used to have pissing contests and I almost always won."

"How...?"

"That's a girl's secret."

"Oh. Why didn't you use the head?"

"It's very noisy, and I didn't want to awaken you. And after all, how intimate is a girl to be on the first date?"

"This is not our first date, I picked up a wet, cold waif and gave her—"

"A sleeping potion!"

"No, it was mint tea."

"I know, go back to sleep."

What Is, Isn't

Annie woke to the smell of coffee and saw a mug, sugar, and canned milk set out. She had had a great night's sleep; the gentle rocking of the boat, and it was good to sleep in the arms of a man again. Taking her coffee out on deck, she found David sitting in the cockpit looking out at Mt. Tam in the distance.

"Why do you look so glum?"

"Who, me?"

"Yeah. I had a great night. You pissed because we didn't have sex?"

"No, I mean I would have liked to, but that's not it..."

"Well?"

David looked away from the distant mountain, and studying Annie very carefully, said, "To be completely honest with you, I am a total basket case. I have never felt this way about a woman. I have thought that I was in love before, but it was not like this. I hardly know you, and yet, I feel that somehow we are a part of each other. I don't know how old you are, or what religious orientation, or if you like kids, or..."

"I'm pushing thirty and yes I would like to have children. So, why so glum?"

"Well, I was living with this woman, and..."

"What was her name?"

"Valerie. Valerie and I were in love, lots of passion, but after a while we stopped talking about getting married, and we fought a lot. Then we would make up with lots of passion, but it was never the same. I always felt that there was something missing; that the connection was frayed or broken. When I talked with my friends about it, they would say, "That's the way it is. What is, is." Well, I think that what 'is,' isn't. I think that there's more to a relationship than loving, breaking up, loving, breaking up. Then one day we were arguing. I said her name, but accidentally called her 'Valkerie.'

"You mean the nasty, feminine something of the Wagner opera?"

"Exactly! And she threw me out."

"Uh, oh."

"So, I guess I'm scared that you and I will fall in love and then have a fight, and the connection will never quite be the same."

"You're afraid to make a commitment?"

"No, not at all! I'm afraid of dying of a broken heart."

"That sounds pretty melodramatic."

Annie moved to sit next to David, placed her hand on his knee, and said, "But it sounds honest, and very sweet." She kissed him on the cheek. David turned to put his arms around her, but bumped her coffee, which splashed onto her/his sweatsuit.

"It's okay."

Annie sat her cup down and pulling up the knees of the baggy sweatpants, straddled his lap facing him. She put her arms around his neck and kissed him. It didn't take long for David to become fully erect, even though this time it was not only tangled in his shorts but rising against the soft weight on his lap. Annie whispered in his ear,

"Why didn't you make love to me last night?"

"On the first date?"

"But you said this was not our first date."

"Uh, because you fell asleep?"

"I'm not asleep now."

"Uh, um."

"David, I've been trying to put into words how I feel about you and us, but I can't find the words. Sometimes words just aren't enough to... um, aren't complex enough to express what one really feels. All I can say is that my heart wants you, my head wants you, and this wants you," Annie said with a wiggle of her hips. "I want to merge with you, have us slide inside each other, I want to conceive a child with you. okay?"

David couldn't speak for a minute, his thoughts, his heart, his mind were racing.

"Well? Was it Zorba the Greek that said it was a sin to turn down the invitation to a woman's bed?"

"AHHHHH! My head says 'take it slow and easy,' my heart says 'Yes, Yes,' and my cock says 'YEAH, YEAH, YEAH! whatever it takes, but do it NOW!"

"I like that. I think your cock and I should continue this conversation." With that, Annie stood up and pulled David down into the cabin.

Annie rolled over in bed. "Let's take a break, I'm kinda sore, I'm a bit out of shape, you know, out of practice."

"Me too. And right now I'm really hungry. Let's go up and get something to eat."

"I can't go like this, my clothes are a mess and this sweatsuit is too big."

"Okay, I'll go and bring something back."

David jumped off the boat and ran up to the coffee house. It wasn't until he was at the cashier that he realized that he was holding up his pants with one hand and that he had left his belt and wallet back on the boat. Fortunately, the girl behind the counter knew him and extended credit. He had flirted with her a few times but then found that she had a girlfriend. At first, he felt a challenge to change her mind but then decided that wasn't going to happen. She seemed to like that he still wanted to be friends. It was a bit of a balancing act to carry the paper tray with orange juice, croissants, morning buns, cheesecake, and hold up his pants with the other hand. He was actually running down the dock thinking, Oh, I hope she hasn't left again!

"Ah, you're back, umm, looks good! You got a call on your mobile phone. I hope you don't mind, but I answered it. I've never used one of these new phones."

"Who was it?"

"Your mom."

"Whoa! Did you talk to her?"

"Sure, about you."

"Oh, come on," says David. "You don't know my mom; I'll never live this down."

"Good… David, have you been dating married women? Because after going through the *Annie Too* stuff, she asked me if I was married."

"And what did you say?"

"No, I've never been married, and I don't have any kids."

"Right, that's what she was really asking. You see, Mom's been after me to get married and says that if I don't hurry up, the only women left will be divorced with a ton of kids. I guess I better call her back, unless there's something else I should know about your conversation?"

"It will keep."

"Tell me, what was it?"

"David, are you a 'mommy's boy'? She said that you hadn't called for about two weeks. How often do you call her?"

"Yes, and a 'father's boy' and a 'sister's boy' and a 'grandpa's boy'. We have a close family, and we're genuinely interested in what the other members are doing. I was just talking with Dad yesterday while I was sailing. We're trying to get Grandpa out on my boat, but he is not in good health and scheduling is difficult. I better call..." He grabbed a few bites of pastry and then dialed. "Hi Mom."

"David, who is that charming woman? How long have you known her? She seems very comfortable with you to be answering your phone."

David was sitting close to Annie, holding the mobile phone so she could hear. "I've known her all my life, and..."

Annie squeezed his knee.

"Where have you been keeping her?"

"Mom, we're pretty busy, haven't eaten breakfast yet."

"Oh, okay. Look, Sis and her family are coming over this afternoon, and grandpa is having one of his good days, so wish you could come up...and bring Annie too. Not your boat! Your lady friend. Bye."

David drank some orange juice, and said with a grin, "I think we have just time for a quickie before we go see my family. You do want to, don't you?"

"Yes and no. I can't meet your family the way I look. I haven't showered, I smell funky, and my clothes are gross. I'm surprised you want to go back to bed again with me the way I look in the light of day."

David picked her up, tried to carry her through the narrow hatch to the cabin below. Both fell onto the cockpit seats, laughing.

"Let's eat breakfast first, then you take a shower up at the restrooms, they even have a hair dryer, I'll hoist your clothes up the mast to catch more wind to dry, and..."

"Not my panties and bra, thank you, I'll wear them damp!"

"I was saying, we'll stop at a department store and find an outfit for you, and maybe I'll pick up a new shirt. I wish I could shower with you."

"We will sometime. Hey, is your place on the way? We could go there, unless you..."

"Good idea! I don't have a hair dryer, but I do have a clean track suit you could wear until we find an outfit for you."

"No problem, my hair will dry on the way. Where are we going?"

"Napa."

"Ahh, a new adventure!"

They quickly ate and cleaned up the cabin, both thinking about that shower. David brought the sleeping bag up on deck to shake it out.

"I'm never going to throw this sleeping bag away; I'll remember our first time..."

"If you don't throw that bag away before the next time I'm on this boat, I'm going to start wearing lots of cheap perfume."

David, covering his face moaned, "Oh no!"

Hearing her laugh, he looked up and tossed the bag on the dock; a corner hung in the water.

Annie had thought that after a quick shower she'd have time to look around David's apartment to get a better idea of who he was, but it was just the opposite. She did learn more about him, but it was in the shower.

Stepping out and standing on the bathmat, Annie felt self-conscious. The sex on the boat has been wonderful, the expression of the passion they had both felt. But here she stood, in the bright glare of the bathroom lights, completely bare ass naked, no clothes and no makeup. She held the large bath towel, drying herself with one hand, while trying to regain some modesty with the other. She turned her back to David. He quickly finished drying himself, stepped closer, and dried Annie's back, hips and legs.

"Do you want me to dry your hair?" asked David

She dropped her towel, turned and embraced him.

"No, thanks," was her answer.

David dressed in linen slacks and a conservative shirt. Annie felt awkward in her borrowed sweatsuit, but David reassured her that they would find just the perfect outfit.

Blue Outfit

David watched Annie as they entered the department store. Her eyes scanned the women's department and stopped at a mannequin wearing a beautiful light blue linen pantsuit. "How about that blue one? It'll look good with your eyes," he said.

Annie felt the fabric, discreetly checking the price tag.

"Oh David, it's beautiful, but I can't afford this much."

"Don't worry, my treat. Tell the clerk your size, and while she's looking, pick up a clean, dry set of undies, and I'll meet you back here."

Annie looked at David, who was smiling, then headed to the lingerie department. *I wonder if he's being bossy or if he's just taking care of a situation.* He seemed very happy to give the gift. Her mother had taught her to graciously accept a gift and not try and say something like, "Oh, it's too much," because that just put the giver in an awkward place. *Well, maybe I could express my gratitude with the way I'm dressed.* She splurged and bought the sexiest "undies," as David called them.

Tingling all over, Annie rushed to the dressing room, where the new outfit hung waiting for her. She couldn't stop smiling. With the door closed, the blue pantsuit seemed to overwhelm the small space. Anxiety gripped her, but she slipped on the blouse. It was too tight across the chest. She couldn't breathe. The room was too small. The blouse felt like a lead weight, just like in her nightmares. Heart racing, she struggled to yank off the blouse with shaky hands.

"You okay in there?" the salesgirl asked.

Annie gulped air, then concentrated on slow deep breaths.

"I'm fine," she said in a wobbly voice. What was wrong with her? She was going to scare David away with these panic attacks.

"Actually, could you please bring me a plain white t-shirt?"

Annie slid on the pants and the jacket; everything fit perfectly. Without the blouse, the outfit was now as comfortable as bib overalls.

She stepped out of the dressing room, unable to stop smiling. She felt like, like... damn, couldn't find the right words. Ever since she met David, her vocabulary seemed so inadequate to express herself and her new feelings. The light blue outfit fit her perfectly, it was so light and cool. But, oh, the white lace on her panties and bra showed through the blue fabric. *Well, it expresses how I feel, and feels so nice against my skin.* She pivoted and twirled around in front of the mirror.

David returned from the men's department while she was doing a little dance. "Oh boy! I wish I were a poet and had a way with words, so I could express how beautiful you are, and how happy you look. That outfit is perfect!"

Annie knew she had made the right choice. He looked handsome in a new dark blue linen shirt, a perfect complement to her outfit, aside from her funky sneakers.

After a quick stop for sandals, they were off to Napa.

Grandpa

David drove past the town of Napa, and on up the valley past rolling vineyards.

"It's so beautiful," Annie said. "I'm used to large, flat fields. In western Kansas, you can stand in the corner of a field, one full mile on each side, a section, and see the other three corners of the field."

"That's really flat," said David. "Grapes do well on rolling hills. They need good drainage."

"Who drinks all this wine?" Annie asked. "Kansas is a dry state, so wine is just not a part of the culture. We even used grape juice in the communion service."

"I don't really know the demographics," David said. "But if one has a good vineyard, with good production and good varieties of grapes, one can do well." He turned off the highway onto a small, paved lane which wound up through scruffy oaks, through a huge vineyard, and out into the yard of a beautiful Victorian house, barn and other outbuildings.

"We're here."

"Wow, your folks live here?"

"Yes, and Grandpa, too, ever since Grandma died eleven years ago. He lives in the converted barn behind the house."

"I remember my grandparents when I was little, but they're all gone now," Annie said. "Mind if I share your grandpa?"

"He would love it! He is hard of hearing and forgets his hearing aid, and he spends much of his time in the past, so those of us who are in the present and future don't always have time for him."

The front door burst open, and people rushed out.

"You must be Annie. Welcome to our home," an elegant grey-haired woman who must be Mom said.

Annie felt the warmth of acceptance as everyone crowded around to greet her. Before all the introductions were made, a little girl of about five ran up and pulled on her hand. "Are you Uncle David's new girlfriend?"

"Yes, my name is Annie, what's yours?"

"Annie Aunt, Annie Aunt, Annie Aunt!" the little girl danced around and around Annie. Her mother Sis corralled her daughter, saying, "Tell Annie your name."

"My name is Pippi Longstocking, and my father is a sea captain sailing the seven seas."

"Last week, she was Princess Leia."

The little girl seemed to stop in midthought. "Oh, what a pretty dress!" She carefully took a little of the fabric in her fingers.

"It's really a pantsuit," said Annie, pulling on the other leg to show the cut of the outfit.

The matching short-sleeved jacket which felt good in the car, was too hot for the Napa Valley. Annie slipped it off and held it out. "Do you want to wear this?"

Sis started to object, but Annie said, "It's okay, it's my gift to her, and look, she's a princess again."

They moved as a happy group into the house, which was cool and smelled of the delicious odors of cooking.

Dad came out of the kitchen wiping his hands on his big, red apron. "Hello, Annie, welcome, I was just taking the biscuits out of the oven. Hope you're hungry. Dinner is about ready."

"Where's Grandpa?" asked David.

"Here I am! Oh, who are you?" asked the old man, coming in pushing a walker.

"I'm Annie."

"Who?" Turning to the group he asked, "What did she say?"

Everyone shouted, "ANNIE!"

"You don't need to shout. I do have my hearing aids in," said Grandpa. "You said Annabelle, right?"

"Well, that's my real name, but no one's called me that since I was about two days old."

"I like that name, I'll call you that," said Grandpa. "Reminds me of something, umm damn, sometimes I think I would forget my head if it weren't attached. Would you sit next to me at dinner and keep an old geezer, I was going to say, 'old fart,' but there are kids around, company?"

"I want to sit next to Annie Aunt."

"As the dad in this family, I should sit next to our new guest, so I can..."

"Hey, she's my girlfriend, and..."

"Annabelle, I asked first, so there," said Grandpa. "If I were a little younger, like a year or eighteen months, I would make a pass at you, but I see that your heart has been captured by David, but I would be honored to have your company for dinner."

Annie, smiling, turned to Dad and said, "Tell me how you irrigate your grape fields?"

"We call them vineyards. We have a pond on the other side of that hill which catches water from a natural spring, so our irrigation is pretty much gravity fed, and that saves on the energy bill. We also use a drip system, which saves water. Why are you so interested in irrigation?"

"I'm from western Kansas, and water is a big item there. My family has about half of their land under irrigation. We're pulling up water from three hundred eighty feet with a thousand-horsepower engine that's pumping a ten-inch pipe and seventy-five pounds per. But the Ogallala Aquifer we're pulling out of is going down. Much of the Great Plains sits on this Aquifer, and no one knows how the water is replaced, or if it even is. It may come from the Rocky Mountains to the west, or it may be pre-historic water just there from eons ago."

"Water is a big issue here, too," Dad said. "How do you know so much?"

"Two of my three brothers farm with my dad, and the third is a hydraulic engineer with a special interest in well water."

"I thought Kansas got their water from windmills," said David. "All the photographs of Kansas have windmills, with beautiful sunsets."

"A lot of homesteads still do use them for domestic water. There's a lot of wind in Kansas. Why, it ain't nothing to see a brick rolling down the road!" Annie said in a soft, western drawl, keeping a straight face.

The three men looked at each other, not quite knowing what to say. Finally, Grandpa said, "Well, maybe rolling sideways, but not end over end."

They all laughed.

"How come you know so much about farming?" Dad asked.

"I'm a tag-along, eight years younger than my youngest brother, and by the time I was sitting at table, three meals a day, I was included in the conversation which was about farming: irrigation, fertilizer, planting schedule, harvest schedule, cattle prices, etcetera, etcetera, etcetera and of course, the weather. If we ran out of farming topics, the meal was pretty quiet except for…'Pass the potatoes.'"

"With your interest in farming, I'm surprised you didn't marry a farmer?" Dad said.

"I grew up on a farm and spent my summers during college helping on the farm. I didn't want to be a farmer's wife."

"Oh, damn!" David said.

"Well, I might just change my mind, there…"

"Oh, GREAT!"

"Yeah, there's this good farmer whose land is next to our family's and he's looking for a wife," Annie said.

"Uuuuuuuuuh." David put his head in his hands.

"But then he's only farming six quarters and we're farming nine quarters," said Annie, smiling.

Grandpa asked, "How large is a quarter?"

"Grandpa, it's not polite to ask how much land a person has," said Dad.

"A quarter is one-fourth of a section," said Annie. "A section is a mile square, which has six hundred and forty acres."

All three men looked at each other, doing the math. David mused, nine quarters is 1440 acres. The Presidio in San Francisco, including the golf course, is 1500 acres.

Dad asked, "What's wrong with one and a half square miles?"

Annie reached under the table and squeezed David's knee. "He's almost fifty and divorced and has a ton of kids."

They chuckled.

Grandpa pushed back his chair. He stood, wobbling. David jumped up to grab his walker.

"Are you okay?" asked David, concerned that Grandpa was slipping into one of his bad days.

"Yes, I've got to get back to my room. Annie, will you help me?"

As she walked with him from the table, someone called out, "Be careful, he's a dirty old man!"

"I'm not so old!" he responded.

They shuffled along the path. Grandpa pointed ahead. "This was the first building on the farm, built by my grandpa. Later, my dad and grandpa built the big house and this became the barn. Now, it's my home."

Inside, Grandpa and Annie settled onto a comfortable sofa. Bookshelves lined the walls, next to beautiful old cabinets filled with treasures behind glass doors.

"Doesn't look like a barn now," she said. "It's really cozy."

"Yeah, I've got my books and junk and I feel very much at home. The kids leave me alone but help when I need. I wish my grandkids would spend more time with me, I have so many stories to tell. Which reminds me, I just remembered about Annabelle, it's over here in one of these books." Grandpa started pulling out scrapbooks and old photo albums, looking at the last pages in each. Annie dozed. She awakened as Grandpa began to talk.

"My Grandpa started these albums. The first entries are at the back of the book, that way current history is placed on top, and you don't have to disturb the old stuff to check out what happened last year. I haven't looked through some of these albums for years. Here's the album with my wife... Oh, shit! Excuse me. I don't want to look at the pictures at the end of her life."

Grandpa turned to the back of the book. "Here she and I are at our wedding. Isn't she beautiful?"

Annie could see that Grandpa was starting to tear up. "Yes, she was beautiful. You miss her a lot."

"Yes, I do. I don't mind growing old so much, I've had a good life and I am comfortable, but sometimes I am very lonely."

Annie put her arm around his shoulders and hugged him. "I asked David if I could share his Grandpa since I don't have any grandparents. I hope that's okay with you."

Grandpa covered his face with his hands and tried not to cry. Annie just held him...He seemed so frail under his shirt.

As soon as he entered the room, David saw what was happening. He sat on the other side of Grandpa and placed his arm around the thin shoulders. Looking at the album, David said, "Oh, it's Grandma. Annie, I wish you could have met her, she was the very best."

The three of them sat for a few minutes, then David said, "Sis is leaving and wants to say goodbye to Annie."

"I really want to hear about Annabelle," Annie said, feeling a sense of urgency.

David and the Rest is History

After her husband and all the kids said goodbye, Sis hugged Annie and said quietly in her ear, "I am so happy for you and David. Mom is going to ask you to stay the night. She wouldn't ask if she didn't like you, so I hope you stay. I have some extra clothes in the guest room which you are welcome to wear, you know, jeans, tennis shoes, and old shirts. There are even 'necessary things' in the bathroom."

Mom did invite Annie to stay and was noticeably relieved and happy that Annie accepted. Mom showed her the guest room and the extra clothes. "We may even put you to work," she said. "I understand that you know a lot about farming."

David entered and said, "You don't have to work if you don't want to. It sounds like we want you to work for your supper."

"If that's the case, I better work for three or four days," said Annie.

David was tempted to say, "Or stay here forever." But instead he asked her to go for a walk. "There's going to be a full moon and I want to show you the moonrise across the pond."

They walked up the path, holding hands. As soon as they were out of sight of the house, they embraced and kissed for a long time. Breaking the embrace, Annie said, "There is something I want to tell you. It won't ruin your evening, but it will let you know where I'm coming from."

David took her hand, and they sat on a bench above the pond. She began by telling him that she had been in a relationship from her junior year in college, and they planned to get married. Her fiancé got a job offer in New York City, so the wedding was delayed until he got established. She loved NYC, all the exciting things to see and do. She found a part-time job, not knowing just how long she would have to work. This left her time to see the city and take some art classes. Doug hated the city. He said you could not see anything for all the tall buildings, and only a part of the sky could be seen. In Kansas, it is so flat that it seems you can see forever, and the sky is as big or bigger than the earth. He also did not like the people, who seemed to always be in such a hurry. One day Doug came home from work and announced that he had accepted a job in Kansas City. He was leaving the next day for a week or so to get the job started. She was to pack up their things and when he returned, they would move to Kansas City. No word was said about getting married, just the move. Annie had no desire to move to Kansas City, which had neither the beauty of the high plains of western Kansas or the excitement of a big city.

That very day, Annie had bought two tickets to Italy, a trip Doug had been promising. Even without a wedding, she thought, they could still have a honeymoon of sorts like they had talked about before. That evening after Doug's announcement, she told him about her plans. Doug got mad and stormed out. They hardly spoke before he left the next morning. Annie packed her things, most of which went into storage, placed Doug's ticket on the kitchen table with a note as to where she would be staying, and left for Italy.

After a few days in Rome, Annie boarded the train to Florence. Even though she felt she appreciated art and had seen good art, it wasn't until she came to Florence that art came alive for her. There had been very little art in her early years in Kansas, mostly Hallmark Card kind of art. But in Florence, art was everywhere in daily life. The second day, she went to see Michelangelo's *David* in the Accademia Gallery. There was a long corridor leading to the *David*, and lining this hall were Michelangelo's *Slaves* sculptures. The figures struggled to emerge from the rough stone. Annie cried when she saw these figures, they looked so much like Doug. She cried for Doug whom she had loved, and she cried for herself for the lost time spent struggling with life. Walking past the *Slaves*, she stood before the *David*.

The impact was more than visual. There was a psychic presence which flooded through her body, touching, embracing the very core of her being. She had to look away. Annie's knees were weak; she reached out to hold the guard rail protecting the sculpture. She turned to look again, her eyes moving up, taking in every detail of the sculpture. Here stood this magnificent man, strong, composed, virile, curly hair, and she knew she wanted a man like that!

At this point in her story, Annie put her arms around David's neck and kissed him. "You are my *David* and I want you."

His kiss told her all she needed to know.

When they reached the pond, the moon was well up, a beautiful moon beam shimmered on the water.

Annie said she needed to finish her story.

In Rome, standing before the *David*, her body shook, tears of joy and of sorrow and of hope wetting her cheeks. An older couple, also teary-eyed, came up and hugged her. The man said this was what art can do, it will touch a person's very center of being.

The couple invited Annie to join them for lunch. Feeling a little lonely and emotionally spent, she accepted. Sitting in an outdoor cafe, Annie, with their encouragement, briefly told them her story. They said she should come to San Francisco; they might have a job for her at MOMA—the Museum of Modern Art.

Annie looked at David. "I never returned to NYC," she said, "And the rest is history."

The Photographer

Early the next morning, Annie slipped out of David's bed and returned to the guest room. She had awakened to the smell of coffee with the sun shining in her face. She loved her new blue outfit, but the jeans, even though they were a little big, felt very comfortable. Mom was still in the kitchen; it was obvious she was just keeping busy waiting Annie's appearance. The two women fell into an easy conversation, both drinking coffee. Annie ate a bowl of fresh fruit and cereal.

"Thanks, Mom, for making me feel so welcome. Your family and home are —"

David burst through the door. "Do you have to go back to the city this morning? Grandpa really wants to see both of us."

"Let's go," Annie. "I'll call in to work."

"Annabelle, I found it, what I remembered!" said Grandpa. "Come over here and sit with me. I'm so very happy that you've come into our lives." He took her hand, holding it tightly. "For a long time I have felt I was through with life, but I guess life was not through with me."

Stacks of albums covered the coffee table. Grandpa picked up the top one but did not open it. "This album was given to me by my granddad just before he died. I loved the old man and spent a great deal of time with him." Turning to David, Grandpa said in a loud whisper, "Hint, hint." David laughed and hugged the older man.

"Well, anyway," Grandpa said, "he would tell me how he came up here to the Valley when land was cheap and started this farm. The whole Bay Area was growing so fast that it was a good market for fresh fruit. He grew cherries, pears, walnuts. Apples didn't do so good, and finally, grapes. He and my dad built the big house. My dad…" Grandpa leaned forward and selected another album from the stack. "Oh, I'm getting off the subject. One day, Grand-dad called me into his office and told me this story. He had been the captain of a boat that hauled hay to San Francisco, but some-thing happened. He sold the boat and came way up here to get as far from the Bay as he could. This was when my dad was still a baby. Well, after he told me this story, he showed me this book and turned to the last page, and as he did, I could see tears in his eyes. I was a young teenager and not used to seeing grown men cry… it left an impression on me."

Grandpa opened the book and there was an old photograph of a couple with a child and a baby. Grandpa pointed to the names written near each person. "Capt'n Jack was my granddad, Susan was my grandmother, and baby John was my dad. But who was 'Annabelle'? My dad never said he had a sister. Grandad told me that she had left but was coming back someday."

Grandpa moved the album so Annie could see the photo-graph. In doing so, the last page lifted, and an old envelope fell out. Grandpa turned the page, and there on the back was the remains of the old glue that had held the envelope. "I never saw this; I thought the photograph was the last entry!"

Grandpa picked up the envelope. It was addressed: TO AN-NABELLE. He turned to Annie. She was staring at the photo-graph, shaking and sobbing.

"David," she said, "that's the man and the boat from my night-mare."

David got up and came around, sitting on the arm of the couch to embrace Annie. He explained the dream to Grandpa. "This boat is a 'scow schooner'," David said, "just like the one you saw from the deck at Sam's. The Alma is a part of the Maritime Museum. Fully restored. It's amazing how similar they look."

The three of them sat for a while. Finally, Annie stopped sobbing.

"What does it mean?"

"Maybe this will explain." Grandpa handed her the envelope.

The letter was written in an old and shaky hand. In a quiet voice, almost a whisper, she read:

The Letter

To Annabelle or whatever you are called.

I am near the end of my life, and I would like the opportunity to once again talk with you as we have so many times when you were young. I know you will come back; I had hoped it would be in my lifetime, but maybe it will be in my grandson's lifetime. I am giving him this letter and photograph and book for safekeeping. I loved your mother very much. She had a fiery personality to match her red hair. She died when you were seven years old. I raised you myself, taking you with me on my boat. You were a wonderful sailor and a great help to me. You could even steer and read the charts.

One Fourth of July, we were all celebrating on the boat. There was no cargo being hauled, so the boat was very light. You were dressed in a pretty new blue dress which you and Susan, my new wife, had made. We were sailing in Raccoon Straits when the weather changed, the fog rolled in, the wind came up very abruptly. The boat was caught in a crosscurrent and jibed.

Having no cargo, the sail was lower, closer to the deck. The boom swung over and knocked you overboard.

I tried to save you! Please believe me! I tried! I cursed that boat for being so slow and clumsy, but I could not find you. We searched for hours until it got dark. For days, I sailed around the shore, looking for you. Your body was never found. Maybe you were washed out to sea. I sold the boat and moved away from the water, but still close enough so that when you came back, you could find me. I told you once that love lasts forever. I know you will come back. My love goes out to you wherever you are.

Your loving father,

Capt'n Jack

The three of them sat in teary amazement.

Finally, Annie said, "I guess this explains a lot." She turned her face, looking at David, smiling through her tears. "Do you think I'm really an incarnation of Annabel?"

"Why not?" said David. "The gods work in mysterious ways. You have appeared here. And I feel like I've known you forever."

"Well, maybe," Annie said. "Are you Capt'n Jack incarnated here and now?"

David shook his head. "Who knows? I certainly love to sail on San Francisco Bay. It's always felt like home."

With a twinkle in her eyes, Annie asked. "Does that make you my father or my brother? Is this incest? Where was your dad the summer of twenty-eight years ago? Did he work the wheat harvest in Western Kansas?"

"No, no, no, and no!" shouted David.

Annie stood and embraced David. "I love you."

David kissed her and said, "I love you, Annabelle, and Annie too."

The End
(Or is it A New Beginning?)

Historical Notes

Capt'n Jack must have had a premonition. Indeed, San Francisco became the center for the new technology of the designing and building of small gasoline engines. With two smaller engines installed, the scows were able to maneuver more easily. They were no longer dependent on the tides. The main mast was removed, and the forward mizzen mast and boom converted to a derrick, which was an aid in loading cargo. More automobiles meant fewer horses, and thus there was less demand for hay and fewer loads to haul. By the late 1890s, the engine conversions were well underway.

Many of the boats were old and worn out and not replaced. Some were reduced to barges and towed. Many of the old scows were left to rot on the banks of the tidal back waters of the Sacramento River delta. One of these hulls was salvaged and lovingly restored to become the ALMA, now moored at the Maritime Museum in San Francisco.

The building of roads and bridges around the growing San Francisco Bay area allowed cargo to be moved by trucks, which were not dependent on docks, wharfs, and waterways. A modern eighteen-wheeler truck can carry twenty to thirty tons. A scow schooner often hauled forty to sixty tons!

During the heyday (no pun intended) of the scow schooner, there were about 400 of these boats working the waters of San Francisco Bay. They were so common that little attention was paid to this unique San Francisco Bay boat. Their passing was almost without notice.

THE RED BOX

Only a small corner was visible, a pile of dirty brown seaweed covered the top and sides of the box. Bright red plastic caught Gray's eye. With a quick flip of his trekking pole, the box was exposed. Picking up and shaking it, Gray determined there was no sea water intrusion, but something bumped around inside. Sunlight and exposure had clouded the plastic. It was impossible to see inside, so there was no communication between the outer world and the hidden secret within.

Gray tried to open the beach treasure, but with only one hand, it refused to allow him access. Frustration and anger flooded his mental state. Gray remembered what his anger management therapist had drilled into him. "Deal with it, it ain't the end of the world." Taking a deep breath, Gray told himself the box was a gift. With thousands of miles of beaches, only he was at the right place at the right time to receive it.

The box was small, but too big to fit in a pocket. Gray could feel his chest starting to tighten. "How am I going to carry this fucking box?" Sometimes he could shove an item under the stub of his left arm, but not today. Not only was the box too big, but the six-inch remnant of his arm was flop, flip, flapping uncontrollably, unable to hold anything. Gray knew this was stress-induced, from his frustration. "Maybe I'll just leave it on the beach, for the next lucky... Naw, can't do that, it's for me."

He shuffled back to his car with the hiking stick stuck through his belt like a pirate's sword, the box in his right hand. The soft sand was hell to traverse without the pole. Ever since the accident, his left hip troubled him on uneven terrain.

Gray sat on an old driftwood log left high on the beach by a storm many years ago. It felt good to give his hip a rest. The bright red box stood out in sharp contrast to the silver-gray surface of the log. Gray stroked the aged wood; its texture added a physical sensation to his perception of its beauty.

He liked his name: Gray. It had been given to him by the two doctors attending his birth, Dr. Gray and Dr. Wilson. His mother disappeared a few hours after the birth. There was a rumor (who knows how it was started) that she was a royal princess from Peru, hiding in America to shed her disgrace. The doctors gave the new infant the best start in life they could, naming him Gray Wilson.

Gray sighed, remembering the auto accident that killed his adoptive parents when he was a teenager, their car hit head-on by a truck. He shook his head. Seemed he had a lot of trouble with vehicles. Gray had moved in with an aunt in Los Angeles.

Arriving at his car at last, he placed the box on the roof, leaned the walking stick against the car near the driver's door, and dug in his pocket for the car keys. Gray had parked his car in the back of the lot, which gave him an incredible view of the beach, the horizon, and sunset.

Settling in, Gray was again appreciative of the comfortable seats in his car. He tried, when he remembered, to find joy or be thankful for little things. This worked... most of the time. The sound of the surf through the open window helped. He closed his eyes and thought about the last few years.

Sitting in the car, memories, one on top of another, crowded into Gray's mind. He tried to focus on his job and the good fortune it brought him, but Sally kept jumping into his thoughts. Would he ever see her again? She had stayed with him for a few days, in the little hospital in the Central Valley after the accident. Then she just disappeared. Took her two boys with her. That had been four years ago.

But when the floodgates of memories (he tried not to go there) were opened, an overabundance of the past rushed in, fighting to be called up into present consciousness. Maybe it was the pain in his hip that triggered the recall of the time in the Central Valley. Closing his eyes, darkness swept in, covering, choking him like a heavy black curtain.

It's dark, very dark. I don't know where I am. It's dark.

I try and remember. The sound of the surf through the open window morphs into a terrifying tidal wave, stretching across the whole horizon. Everyone is running. Or was that a dream? I'm in bed with a very nice, comfortable woman. Not a knockout beauty, but at my age, comfort is the best part of lovemaking. I'm hoping this is not a dream.

"Hello, anyone there?" I ask.

Silence, except the sound of high heels tap, tap, tapping down the long hall to the nurse's station.

Darkness and silence…not a good combination. I'm not afraid. Just a feeling of unease.

Years ago, I hiked down into the Carlsbad Caverns in New Mexico. The guide said the lights would be turned off for a few minutes. "No talking, hold someone's hand," he said. "It'll be so dark you won't be able to see your hand in front of your face." He was right. A few minutes passed, then out of the darkness and silence came a little voice. "Mommy, it's dark in here!" We all laughed and the lights came on.

Where is my guide? Where is my mommy? Where is the light? I'm beginning to feel sensory deprivation. I recall the stories and studies that came out of the Korean War, accounts of torture using this technique. I am not afraid. But the unease is increasing.

There is no pain. That's the good news. Pain cannot be remembered. The incident of pain, the experience, the time and place can be recalled. But the feeling of pain itself cannot be remembered. I have experienced pain; some so intense, I passed out. I am very relieved to not re-experience those body-twisting extremes.

Am I dead? Have I crossed over? I don't think so. I do not believe in an "in-between place" of darkness. If I were dying, I would be following a light. This is a totally new existence. There is no smell. Often there is a new smell with a new experience. The heavy sweet odor of flowers in Hawaii. The dry, dusty, delicious aroma of ripe, dry wheat ready for harvest. And of course, the multiple fragrances arising from the wind-blown sea. Here, there is nothing.

Could this be the physical location of depression? I think not. For me, depression is the lack of light. There is some light, but not enough to play in. It is not black, just dark. So where am I? Depression is often accompanied with the uneasy feeling of emptiness. I feel alive, not desolate or vacant.

Is this the "calm before the storm"? Maybe, but what storm? Looking over my life, I see no storm clouds approaching. Perhaps the storm is the ever-present process of aging. Not really a raging storm, but the increasing difficulty of using my physical body. Oh, yes. My left arm.

Let's not go there. Is it possible? The darkness is becoming darker as I think about my physical condition. But where is the light? If I could just see a glimmer, a tiny pinpoint of light, I could focus and move in that direction.

The amputation wound became infected and more of Gray's arm was removed. "You're lucky to be alive," the doctor said in response to his concern about the amount of arm lost. There were dark days and nights. He knew he was heavily sedated. It was not a good drug trip.

Ten or twelve years ago, he had been a chef in a fried fish restaurant. Long hours, drugs to stay awake and alert. After work, more drugs to relax and sleep. Sally had been with him in those days. Awakening from a three-day stupor, Sally beside him was still out. He knew he had to get off the drugs. Sally did not. She left. Gray got himself cleaned up… clean and sober. Took a job with a remodeling contractor installing kitchen cabinets and natural stone counter tops. He was a good salesman.

One night about eight year later, Gray was awakened at 1 am by knocking. There was Sally, standing in the open door. "I'm out of gas, out of money, and have two kids in the car."

He helped her carry the sleeping boys and tucked them in on the couch. With no explanation, she kissed Gray, took off her clothes and crawled into his bed. They lived together for a few weeks, Gray never knowing if she would be there when he got home in the evening.

They decided to drive to L.A. Gray took a week off, and they headed South, taking the Central Valley route. He had no children, had never been a parent. The constant bickering and whining in the back seat riled him. It was hot. Gray was driving with his left arm on the open windowsill.

"You two, shut up!" he shouted, looking back over his right shoulder.

There's a lot of truck traffic on US 99. Big trucks, eighteen wheelers. The highway is narrow. North and southbound traffic only separated by a double yellow line. The car drifted a little to the left. Gray was able to pull off the highway and stop the car before he passed out. The whole left side of the car, including his arm, was gone.

Gray, with tears in his eyes, stretched in the car seat and pulled himself out of the darkness of memories. The sun was setting. He started the car and pulled out of the parking lot. He did not like revisiting that time in the Central Valley. Usually those thoughts could be diverted, but today...

Today. The walk on the beach. The red box—

"Oh, my God!" he shouted. "I left it on the roof of the car."

A quick check, no box. A frantic drive back to the parking lot, now empty of cars. Approaching his old spot, the headlights illuminated a flash of red. The box, or what was left of it, run over by car tires.

"At least it's open!" Gray laughed.

In the remaining jagged shards of plastic lay a smooth rock. It nestled comfortably in the palm of his hand, the shape of a small egg. The sea-washed stone was made of two minerals. The larger half was a warm, gray stone. Fused on top was a sizable piece of very white quartz. Turning the rock over, Gray could see a dirty, dark smudge, hard to make out in the low light of the car's interior. He spit on the stain and rubbed it with a thumb. It didn't come off.

"Must have been from an oil spill," said Gray. "Nope, the box had a good seal. I know, it must have come from the tire that ran over and broke the box."

Time seemed to stand still. The parking lot was very empty. Gray felt tears welling up in his chest. His eyes teared.

"Help me," he mumbled out loud.

Gray heard, or felt, or sensed, a quiet voice say, "The box is a gift. Make it your own."

A few minutes of tears, the welcome release of pain. Gray sniffed and wiped his nose on his left shirt sleeve. He laughed, realizing he only had a few inches of sleeve, but it was just enough to wipe his nose and the streaks of tears on his cheeks.

"This is my reality. I only have one arm, but enough sleeve on the other to wipe my nose." He continued to laugh.

With a rush, the meaning, the gift of the fiery red box became obvious. Of course, the gray stone was himself, trapped inside a world of anger. The box had been sealed. No wetness, no healing bath of sea water could reach him.

Again a tire had violently shattered his world. First, it had taken his parents, then his left arm. Finally, it had deposited a stain on his life when it broke open the box. But now he could see above the gray stone, beautiful, pure white quartz. A capstone. Permanently fused together from its time of origin millions of years ago. Like an egg, promising new life, it would bring Gray a sense of balance, clarity, and spiritual wellbeing.

He carries the stone in his pocket. For help.

A touchstone.

HERE AND THERE

Color, colors, bright, vivid color. Some I have never seen before. Images shift, each more compelling. Some I recognize. Mighty rust red sandstone arching above me, silhouetted against the intense blue sky of Utah. The sky above morphing into the deep blue waters of Puget Sound on a bright, sunny day in the Pacific Northwest. In the distance, Mt. Baker floats above a thin line of dark green forest on the horizon. The blue surrounds me, covering me. All I can see is blue, as if I'm standing too close to a watercolor painting, my eyes recording only the blue of a flower petal, none of the design.

"Where am I?"

Silence.

"What's going on? Anyone there?"

"You are," comes the answer.

"Who said that?"

"You did."

I look around, still in a slowly pulsating, protective blue glow. I see no one, I don't even see myself. For some reason, I don't feel frightened, there is no discomfort. I actually feel great, there is a sense of well-being, and curiosity. A slow smile builds. My spirit guide often comes with a blue presence.

"If I said that, who is this 'I' talking?" I ask. "I'm confused."

"Of course you are. I will explain."

"Thanks."

"You already know from your mediation that you, we, us, are the combination of a non-physical being and its physical manifestation. The part that walks around in the physical world. That's its part. You, we, are now back together in the non-physical world. The physical body is no longer, its job is done. And I might add, well done."

"Whew! That means I have crossed over," I exclaim.

"Yes."

"Then why am I still having a conversation with…"

"Because the you that just arrived has not completely made the transition to integrate back into one soul on this side."

"Oh, how…?"

"It takes practice. There will be guidance. The residual you is progressing comfortably. The crossing over is going well. Some beings have difficulty… oh well, let's not go there."

"How long does it take?"

"Ah ha, there is no dimension of 'time' over here."

"Will I have a job? I don't want to just sit around. I love to work… or play, as I used to call it when there was creativity involved."

"Oh yes, just as both aspects of us co-created in the physical world, now that we are one, there is very much creativity to do."

"Great! Will we be creating side-by-side with God?"

Silence.

"What happened?"

"Your concept of 'God' is going to be… shall I say, modified."

"Hmm…"

"Here comes a guide. It feels good to be one again."

I see (I think I can see) a beautiful cinnamon glow coming.

"Is that you, Leo, my dog Leo?"

"Yes," says Leo. "And some of the dogs you have had before. We're your guide and companion as you adjust to this world."

"That feels very good," I say.

"Remember when I crossed over?" says Leo. "You built an altar at my favorite window seat. Each morning you meditated there and encouraged me to go on into the light. I didn't want to go… I was only eight, in the prime of life. You really helped. I was able to rejoin with my spirit self after just a few days."

"Yeah, I remember," I say. "Your spirit and I had quite a conversation. My questions were about the other side."

"Yes," says Leo. "I'm an old soul."

"I asked why you chose a dog's body to incarnate. You answered, 'Look at the body your spirit chose.' Ha!"

We both laughed.

"Yes," said Leo, "You never answered that question."

"I'm very happy you're here to help me," I say.

"Yes, me too. That's me, Me Too. Remember me? When you were a kid, everyone liked me for the beautiful puppies I sired. But you… you loved me. We were buddies, companions. I even slept on your bed."

"Of course," I say. "You were a friend."

"We are all here," he says. "One spirit, with different physical world selves, at different times in your earth life."

"I feel tears," I say. "But I think they're tears of joy. I'm very glad we are all together again. I've got a question."

"What?"

"Does your spirit self, being an animal, exist like us humans?"

"Yes and no. Most animals, in their earthy physical form, are very connected with their spirit self. When they cross over, they quickly turn around and go back to the physical world."

"So, why are you still here?" I ask.

"It's hard to explain. When there is love between a physical human and a physical dog, they, how do I say it? Create a bond on the spiritual side. So, here we are. We are a part of your guidance program. You are doing very well. I'm tempted to say, 'Good Boy.'"

"I got it." I laugh. "Do I get a treat? How about other animals?"

"Definitely a treat! You will see it when you complete the transition. Other animals I have seen, not really seen, observed, or perceived are horses and a few others."

"How about cats?" I ask.

Silence

"Well...?"

"Let's not go there."

YIP YIP YIP

I think I see him (or her) out there, behind the sage bush next to the Joshua Tree. I don't really see him. It's a movement, a brown/gray ghost blending within all the brown gray of the desert. It's almost dark, no moon tonight. I have a visitor.

This visitor, this gray ghost, is silent. Earlier, while the low sun was playing with the trees making long shadows, there came the greeting song, "Yip, yip, yip, aowwww!" The final sounds breaking into falsetto. Primordial sounds that bring cold shivers and a quickening heartbeat.

I howl in reply. My greeting is pathetic, the best I can do. It came out more like the onomatopoeic "howl" sound. Nothing resembling the beautiful, haunting song of the desert coyote. My message, I hoped, conveyed that there was no food in my car to share. An earlier dinner in a small town outside Joshua Tree National Park, no leftovers, and only a full thermos of hot coffee for breakfast meant no food for him. There is some fresh fruit in a locked cooler. Tomorrow, after my last morning coffee, I will start a few days of fruit-fasting and meditating. I hope my visitor will understand.

Walking out into the desert night, I turn around twice with my eyes closed. I'm totally lost. The North Star is easily found, but I had not walked away from my camp with the star in mind. There's no reference orientation. Faint signs of panic creep into my chest.

"This is ridiculous," I say with a shake of my head. "I've got a flashlight in my pocket. It's just an experiment." It is working. I finally admit to myself that this trip to the desert is all about being alone. Returning to my car (with the help of the flashlight), I spread out the ground cloth and unroll my pad and sleeping bag.

This is the fourth time I have answered the call to come to the desert to meditate. The first time, I brought a tent. It was not needed. The second visit it snowed. I stayed in a motel in town. The last time, in the night the full moon came up, painting everything silver-blue-white. She had loved this, her first visit to the desert. But that was a long three years ago. Now, with the help of dark nights and daily meditations, I hoped an answer would emerge to settle my heart. I needed that.

She came with me to the desert to experience first-hand my joy and connection with its natural healing power. It worked. We made love in the moonlight, its radiance glistening in the moisture on our bodies. Long day walks across the vastness of the desert were punctuated by laying down to rest on the soft sand at the bottom of dry creek beds. After napping and lovemaking, we sat on a rock outcropping and meditated together. No need for a spoken mantra to become centered. The desert was there, in the sounds of the wind whispering through the cactus needles and in the complex odors it brought along.

We were one. Our lovemaking became our life-making.

The details of life could be worked out over time as needed. We were co-creating all of us, our physical selves, and our non-physical selves.

What happened?

I snuggle into bed. I try to meditate, but the monkey chatter in my brain is too loud. I keep thinking of her and of our time here years ago. This may even be the same spot we camped. My chest tightens, then my throat. Tears. My cheeks are wet. A sound struggles out from somewhere deep inside me, a mournful coyote call. Blessed sleep takes me, wrapping me in its gentle arms.

I awaken, my face very wet. This is more than tears…it's rain! Should I creep into my car? It's not very comfortable trying to sleep in the back seat. Grabbing the edge of my ground cloth, I roll over, covering myself. The rain is very light and with it comes the intoxicating smell of petrichor, the powerful odor of new rain on dry rocks and soil.

The morning sun quickly dries the rocks and my sleeping tarp. Breakfast is tepid coffee and fruit. I set out on a morning walk. Surrounding me are blankets of color, spread out to the horizon. Looking down, there is not much to see. Individual flowers are so minuscule, sprouting up from the cracks between stones. Bursting out from a tiny seed waiting there for a drop of rain to start new life. Shifting my eyes out over the distance, the colors are intense. A gentle breeze gives movement to this vast canvas of color. Not the great, rolling ocean-like waves in a ripening wheat field on the prairie, but little, quick dancing steps of a chorus ensemble, all in sync.

I love the high desert, its harsh beauty, its vastness, and the room for my loneliness. I am alone; no humans in sight, no sounds of civilization, nothing to distract me from fully experiencing my emotions. My movements are a walking meditation, I'm at one with my world. Laying down on the soft sand in the bottom of a dry creek bed puts me even closer to the earth. This is good. Healing is taking place. I drift off to sleep with a smile on my face.

What awakened me? I try to remember where I am. There is a dull ache in my head. Looking around, I don't see my car, but there is the rock outcropping I remember being parked near. The walk back is not pleasant, too much sun, and too much soft sand. Next time, I'll try to stay on a path.

By the time I arrive back at my camp and car, a headache is pounding in my ears. My loneliness is devouring me. This desert trip was to help me come to terms with myself and moving on. But the more I meditate the more painful it becomes.

Rummaging around in the glove box, I find some ibuprofen. Opening a new bottle of water from the ice chest and drinking deeply, the cold hurts my sinuses. Setting still for a while helps. I know I am allowing my emotions to helplessly drag me around through my desolate internal landscape.

"Get ahold of yourself," I say out loud. "Use the techniques you've learned. Breathe. Focus on the light."

It's later than I realize. Supper is a banana, then a second one. Maybe my headache is from caffeine withdrawal. By this time of day, I usually have had three or four mugs of that rich, dark brown aroma-laden gift from the gods. Maybe this fruit fast is not the best way to examine myself. I wish I had a cup of coffee.

Just as blessed sleep is creeping over me, another car pulls into the parking lot. I'm surprised. There had been only one car passing the pull off to this rock outcropping this morning, none this afternoon. My car is parked far to the right side of the lot, away from the trail leading to the rocks. The car's headlights swing towards me, pause, illuminating my car, then continue to the other end of the lot.

At first, I'm annoyed. This is my spot, my special spot. But they are quiet, and I start to drift off again. They light a lantern, not really a problem, just a reminder of their presence. Sleep slips in again, when I hear music.

"Oh, crap! Now what? Why don't they use headphones?"

A gentle breeze blows the sound towards me.

Then I hear it.

"Oh, my God. It's Samuel Barber—my favorite." I relax and listen to the beautiful, and hauntingly moving Adagio for Strings & Voice by Samuel Barber. My body relaxes, my tumultuous emotions quiet down. Breathing becomes deep and regular.

The music comes to a crescendo of very high, almost shrill tones. Just next to me, not fifty feet away, a voice joins in with a spine tingling "Awoooooooooah". What a wonderful gift: Samuel Barber and a desert coyote. I wish the concert would keep playing. No lights, and all is quiet from the other car. Never again will hear that Adagio without also hearing the desert coyote's solo.

"Hello, anyone awake?" comes a voice.

Opening my eyes, I think I'm still asleep, still dreaming. Rolling over, I can make out a figure walking towards me. It is a woman. She is wearing a very large sun hat, can't quite make out her face, a white blouse and beige pants; the kind with lots of pockets. I still can't make out her face. In her hand is a large bag.

I get up and pull on my jeans.

"Oh, sorry," she says. "I didn't know you were still asleep. I'll come back later."

"No. No. This is fine."

"Are you alone?" she asks.

"Yea, I'm alone, very alone."

"I meant, are you by yourself?"

"It's okay," I say. "Come on over."

She steps around the car to my meager camp.

"I, ah, um, just wondered if I could borrow a, uh, some drinking water?"

"Of course."

"I was making coffee and my water bottle fell over."

She explains it was the last of her water supply, she's leaving today, but doesn't want to be in the desert without water.

"So, you saved the coffee and sacrificed the water."

She grins. "Yeah, that's about right, I have—"

"Good choice," I say.

Setting down and opening her bag, she pulls out a large thermos bottle. "I could trade you a cup of coffee for the water."

"Well," I say, "I'm on a fruit fast, trying to cut down on my caffeine intake."

"Oh, I'm sorry, I—"

"However," I say with a grin, "it has been 24 hours. I think it's time to break my fast and declare a victory."

"Fantastic! Let's celebrate your success. I also have some half 'n half and sugar. What's your pleasure?"

My camp is very sparse, just my bed roll and ice chest. She sets the coffee service, including two mugs, on top of the chest. I go to the car and bring back two folding camp chairs.

"Two chairs?" she observes.

"I stored my camping gear three years ago. Haven't used it since. Guess I just loaded everything in the car."

As I unfold the second chair, I feel a knot gripping my chest and throat. Turning away so she can't see my emotion, I cover my face with my hands.

She touches my arm. I feel a rush. Goosebumps rise on my bare arm.

"And now she's not here," she says quietly.

I let out a deep sob and collapse into a chair.

"How did you know?" I ask.

"I'm a woman. We know such things." She pours the coffee, adding cream and sugar, and hands me a warm mug. Reaching in her bag, she pulls out two granola bars. Perfect with the coffee. We sit in silence, enjoying the moment of sharing.

"Do you want to talk about it?" she asks.

"Nope, I hardly know you, not even your name."

"I'm Bethany. I'm here if you want."

We continue to sit in silence, thinking.

I clear my throat; the coffee is comforting. "Bethany's a beautiful name, very midwest. Are you from there?" I ask.

"Yes, Nebraska."

"Do you know the meaning of 'Bethany'?" I ask.

"Yes," Bethany says. "Do you? And what's your name?"

"Oh, sorry, it's John. Also a good midwestern name. Let me see if I can remember." I think for a while, trying to recall my book of symbols. "Oh yes, Bethany, the ancient town, is the place where crossings are made, one side to the other." I pause. "Adversity and discomfort are turned into good times."

"You got it." Bethany smiles, lifting the brim of her sun hat. I see her eyes and hair for the first time, bright in the morning sun, eyes of many colors. Eyes of brown with flecks of gold and green. Her hair, glowing gold-red-brown, fills my senses with a thrill. She returns my focused stare and smiles. We don't move, just looking. My brain is racing with thoughts, and images, fantasies of us together. I wonder if she is also…

"Let's go for a walk, she says. "You ready?"

"No, let's have some fruit." I open the ice chest.

"Oh, my God! I'm so hungry for fresh fruit. Just look at those plums, and grapes, too."

"My favorite also, organic, seedless."

We clean up, I have another cup of coffee. It is the best.

I put on a shirt with sleeves, find my hat, and we walk out into the desert. When the path becomes rocky or difficult, Bethany puts her hand into mine. It just seems like the natural thing to do. I look at her, she does not return my gaze. Walking over a ridge and down into a small valley, we lay down on the soft sand of a dry riverbed for a nap. Awakening, I say that I want to tell her something. "You are the first woman I have said this to. I am a widower, and I am lonely."

I explain how I tried a number of times to make a meaningful connection through a dating service. Didn't work. Never got beyond, "I'm a widower." The rest never got spoken.

"Thanks for trusting me," Bethany says. "Do you want to talk more about your loneliness?"

"Maybe later."

It's late when we return to camp. Bethany offers to make dinner; she still has some camping food left. After dinner we lay down on my sleeping bag, cuddling close because of the chill. Maybe because it's dark, or that I didn't have to look her in the eyes, I begin to tell her my story. Feeling her close gives me the support to speak the truth.

We had been together for 40 years. I knew something was not right, but she didn't want to talk about it. We came to the desert, maybe this very spot. The first night was wonderful. The second afternoon she was in great pain. She told me she was dying. We talked. The next morning she was not in bed with me. I found her curled up in the back seat of the car, a note pinned to the blanket she had rolled herself in. It said, "Thanks for the lifetime of love." I drove the body to town. The hospital took care of everything.

Bethany doesn't speak for a long time. "Thanks for sharing your pain with me. I would like to bring my sleeping bag here and zip them together if it works. Would you mind if I play the Samuel Barber music?"

The bags zip together. We slip in and listen to the recorded music. Not just one, but two coyotes join the music with their own notes. It's miraculous.

I turn to Bethany and say, "Looks like the coyotes have found their mates." I reach over and attempt to pull her closer. She raises herself on an elbow, kisses me, and says, "I do not want to make love. I mean I do, and I don't. I'm so funky. I've been camping for a week without a shower."

We lay back, side by side, looking up at the sparkling dome overhead listening to the coyotes sing. I awake in the night; she's pressed against me, her head on my chest. The feeling of wholeness has entered my body and my psyche. The process of transformation, of crossing, of Bethany is settling into a new way. I wonder how much more I have to do; the process is ongoing.

The morning activities, including breakfast, flow smoothly. The coffee's delicious. Bethany's first words are, "That's the last of the half 'n half. I need to be on my way today. I've been here a day longer than planned."

"Thanks for staying," I say. "Our talking was… was just what I needed. And our 'lovemaking' cuddle last night left me feeling… well, feeling loved."

"Me too. I loved you holding me. I, too, feel loved."

We shuffle around clearing up, both feeling a little embarrassed for speaking out so honesty about love. Bethany faces me, holding my arms. She looks deep into my eyes. "You still have some work to do. Now's a good time to continue your process."

"What do I have to do?" I ask.

"I saw the small wooden box in the back of your car. Your wife's ashes?"

I nod.

"You brought them to this special place. You must toss her ashes into the wind over the desert. This is for you, not her. She is not the ashes, but has already left, crossed over to her new life on the other side."

I shuffle my feet.

"You need to let her go, to help her break the bonds with her physical earth existence. Bonds you're still holding. She has work to do on the other side."

I feel healing energy flowing into my whole being from Bethany's hands, through her touch. She pulls me into a hug.

"Go now," she says. "Go into the desert and empty the little box. I will be gone when you return."

"But I haven't heard your story. I've been so selfish, not listening, not hearing you."

Bethany shakes her head. "It's okay. I'm good. This has been your time, your transition, your Bethany. Go now, knowing you are loved."

Holding the little box, I stumble out into the desert, my face wet with tears. The breeze freshens, the wind comes up whistling through the cactus needles. With the gusts at my back, I toss the fine, gray ashes up and up into the air to be carried away, dissipating, dissolving, disappearing. For a brief moment, each speck of ash dust sparkles in the desert sun.

"Follow the light," I say, a smile in my voice.

I walk back towards my car, and around the rock outcropping. When the parking area comes into view, I stumble only once, but quickly recover.

Bethany's car is gone.

BELOW THE BRIDGE

The wind is howling in from the sea. The gusts make it difficult for some to zip up their windbreakers.

I love coming here, thinks Charles. *The heated seats in my new car feel very comfortable. I'm right here surrounded by the wind, the waves pounding as they crash on the rocks below me. The surfers are enjoying the big waves today. Glad I'm not out there.*

Even with the windows rolled up, Charles hears a new sound, not present at his previous visit. It is a low moan, increasing and decreasing in intensity, occasionally jumping an octave. The railings on the pedestrian walkway above have been replaced. The vertical slats on the new railing, with a different design, reduce wind load on the bridge, but now they sing in a low moan. This new sound mixes with the bump/thump, bump/thump, thump/thump as cars roll over the expansion joints in the bridge deck overhead.

The fog has not yet crowded its way into San Francisco Bay, but Charles knows that with this wind it will not be long. The sun is still shining, illuminating the vivid rust-red paint on the complex steel of the bridge. Even as he studies the south tower rising imposingly above him, the very top is beginning to disappear in the encroaching fog. Charles lowers his view to the old fort, built during the Civil War to protect the valuable gold and silver mines in the mountains to the east of San Francisco. It is framed by an arch of red steel, incorporated in the bridge itself. The fort, a state-of-the-art design, with massive, thick walls and row upon row of cannon ports, was never finished. The war was over and its armaments had become obsolete.

Charles's view is interrupted by a person walking past his driver's side window. She disappears, dropping out of sight. She must have fallen. Charles jumps out of the car, the wind slamming his door shut. She is sprawled on the concrete, holding her left knee. He kneels.

"You've fallen," he says. "Did you bump your head?"

There is no response from the woman.

"I must ask you some questions," he says. "You may be hurt, but I need to know if you hit your head."

She turns her pain-contorted face to him and slowly shakes her head.

"Can you sit up? Here," says Charles. "Let me help."

He takes her right hand, and she rolls up to a seated position.

"Are you dizzy?" he asks. "I must know if you hit your head. Take your right hand and feel your head."

She rubs her head. "It's okay, just my knee hurts like hell."

"That's good. Can you see the bridge? Is it moving?

She looks up, blinks her eyes. "Nope, it's steady."

"Now I want you to follow my finger with your eyes." He holds up his finger.

She tilts her head back, but looks into his face, not at his finger.

Something like a gust of wind buffets Charles. *These are the most beautiful eyes I have ever seen,* he thinks. *Green with flashes of brown and even blue.*

"You are not moving your finger," she says.

Charles recovers and moves his finger slowly left and right. She follows the movement, with a smile on her face.

"Okay," he says. "I guess we don't need to call an ambulance. But we do need to look at that knee." He stands up, becoming aware of his own knees hurting from kneeling on the rough pavement.

"I'll get some water from the car to wash your knee." Charles stops, takes off his jacket. "Here, put this on. You look cold." He helps her find the arm holes in the too-large garment.

"Thanks, this really feels good. I'm pretty cold."

Charles returns with a water bottle and a towel. "Can you stand? You can lean on the front of my car." He starts to reach out but stops and says, "I can help you up, but I will have to touch you. Is that okay?" He looks around, but everyone, except an old van at the far end, has left the viewpoint parking lot. The cold fog continues to roll in.

"Of course, just be careful of my knee."

Charles embraces her and very quickly leans her against the hood of his car. "You need to bend your knee, to see if it's broken."

"Oh, ow! That hurts."

"Is the pain inside or on the surface?"

"Can't tell."

Charles bends down and gently holds her leg. He is focused on the knee, but feels her hand on his neck, supporting herself. He slowly bends her knee. It works okay.

"This may sting when I wash the wound, so if you can, you should do the washing yourself."

"I'll try, but you hold me so I don't tip over."

Charles slips one arm around her and with his other hand pulls up the cuff of her long shorts to clean the wound. An ugly scar runs along her thigh and up under her shorts.

"You're not from around here, are you?" He says, trying to distract her from the pain.

"Ohhh. No, how did you know? oh oh ohhh."

"Locals don't wear shorts in summer. Too cold."

"Oh boy, oh, oh. You got that right. Oh, shit!"

Charles leans down and inspects the knee. "Looks good and clean. Glad it's not any worse. Looks like that leg has had a ton of trauma already."

"Yes, sometimes it doesn't work right. The foot doesn't come up, and I trip."

"Yeah, I can see that. There's a wheel stop next to the car you must've tripped over. Now let's get you warmed up." He helps her into his car.

"I'm sorry to be taking so much of your time—"

"Nothing I'd rather do than rescue a maiden in distress." Charles bows, doffing an imaginary hat.

"Well, thanks. Your car is so nice and warm. I feel better already," she says. "How come you know so much first aid?"

"I studied to be an EMT, but I stopped."

"Why?" she asks. "You seem so good at it."

"I get squeamish at the sight of blood." Charles says with a grin.

"Oh, come on…" she says. "What's your name?

"Charles, and yours?"

"Mary."

"No way," laughs Charles. "Every picture of her I've seen, she had blonde hair. Not the beautiful black hair that you have."

"Oh, God," Mary replies, reaching for the door handle. "You are either flirting with me, or full of B.S., or your knowledge of art is—"

"Maybe all the above," says Charles. "Let's go get a cup of coffee. I know of a 'Warming Hut' not far from here."

"Well, I guess it's okay. It would be nice to warm up inside. Is it safe leaving my car here?" says Mary. She glances around the parking lot. "Go, go now!" she cries. "I don't want them to see me."

Charles quickly backs around to leave, wondering what scared her. The rearview mirror reveals a few surfers dressed in wetsuits, heading to a beat-up van. "The surfers?"

"Yes, but I don't want to talk about it now."

The Warming Hut was just that, nothing fancy, just good hot coffee and delicious pastries. They sat, looking out at the Bay and the Golden Gate Bridge rapidly being wrapped in white. The center span foghorn sounded its deep "OHMMMMM."

"I love that sound," says Charles. "Seems almost like a prayer to warn sailors."

"Do you know the Sufi chant Om Shri Ram?" asks Mary.

Joining the next horn blast, Mary adds the chant to the powerful "OHMMMMM" of the foghorn. "Om Shri Ram Jai Ram Jai Jai Ram…"

They join in a sing along with the foghorn and the "Om."

"The chant brings us closer to the Divine," she says.

"Are you from India?" asks Charles.

"Kinda." Mary laughs. "My grandmother was Indian, married to an English man. My mother was raised in India but went to England for college where she met my father, an American. I was born and raised here. I'm American."

"This is beginning to get interesting," says Charles. "I'm wondering, where do we go from here with this story? You know, 'Boy meets Girl'…"

"Or 'Girl meets Boy.'"

"Well, yeah…" says Charles. "I still don't know why you were so frightened by the surfers in the parking lot. And what's the story about the scar on your left leg?"

Mary doesn't respond, just looks at Charles with a faint smile. "One possibility. You could drive me back to my car," says Mary. "We say 'goodbye', and we each drive away." She takes her last sip of coffee. "The end."

"Hell no!" says Charles. "I would probably drive on the freeway, distracted by thinking about you, and I'd have an accident and die in the wreckage."

"That sounds overly dramatic," says Mary. "So, let's have dinner tonight. I know a good Indian restaurant."

"Okay, but we can't just end the story there."

"Well, after dinner, we could go back to your place or mine, and, you know, make love."

"Sounds good to me."

"But I'm afraid that when I undress, you will see my scar and lose your desire for me."

"No way…"

"It's pretty ugly, no blood, but it's gross."

"Okay, we'll do it in the dark."

"That sounds scary. I think we should just forget that sex scene in the story."

Charles pushes back his chair. "Whatever. Time for me to take you back to your car."

Outside the Warming Hut, Charles opens the car door for Mary. "I have another idea for this story."

"What?" she asks.

He pauses, trying to find the right words. "We could meet tomorrow morning, maybe for breakfast. Spend the day together and see if we are compatible. Then, if we go to bed together, it would ...well, you know..."

Mary squeezes his hand. "You're sweet."

Driving to the Fort parking lot, Charles asks Mary, "Why were you so frightened of the surfers?"

"My brother died while surfing. I think he was murdered, and I'm here in San Francisco looking for answers."

Charles slows the car very quickly and backs up about a hundred feet, starting forward again.

"What are you doing?" asks Mary.

"This is a do-over. I don't want this story to be a murder mystery. I know it's important to you, but I don't want to go there."

"So, if that's the way you feel," says Mary in a huff, "we'll just get in our cars and drive away. End of story."

They remain silent on the way back to the parking area.

He pulls in. There are only two cars there, Mary's and another parked very close. Mary utters a little shriek and slips down to the floor, hiding.

"Don't let them see me," she says. "Please don't!"

A man who was crouched behind Mary's car straightens up and watches as Charles drives past, parking at the far end of the lot near the fort. He watches as the man and car are backing out to leave. On the side of the car are the words: Park Presidio Police.

Charles drives back and parks next to Mary's car. "It was the Park Police. Probably just checking an empty car."

"See ya tomorrow," says Mary, flipping her hair as she opens her door, making no reply to his information.

"About ten, here?" asks Charles.

She nods, turns and gets in her car and drives away, disappearing in the fog.

Charles arrives about nine the next morning and parks near the surfers. The waves are huge, rolling in from the ocean, dashing themselves against the jagged boulders of the sea wall protecting the old fort. He watches as the surfers ride the waves in, diving off their boards just before their ride slams into destruction. No sandy beach here.

A surfer struggles out of the water and up the rough rocks, dragging his board along. It's hard work. These are no ordinary stones, softened by thousand of years in a river. They were dynamited out of a quarry wall high in the Sierra Mountains. These raw boulders with the sharp, jagged edges form the imposing water breaker, the killer of waves. Once the waves have smashed into the rocks and spent themselves, they still try and wash the surfer and his board back into the sea. The surfer makes it to the top of the wall and collapses.

"Are you okay?" asks Charles, kneeling beside him.

"Yeah, just tired."

"Looks like a hell of a place to surf!"

"Yeah… it's a challenge, but close to the City."

"Do you know of a surfer who died here recently?"

The surfer rubs his face. "That was Robert. Surf was really high that day. He didn't get off his ride soon enough and smashed into the rocks. We had trouble getting him out."

The surfer looks out at the waves breaking below.

"These rocks are killers. He was beat to a pulp. Bad."

"Does he have a sister?" asks Charles.

"Yeah, Mary. She's crazier'n bat shit. Thinks her brother was murdered. Won't let it go."

"Was she surfing that day?" asks Charles.

"No, she hasn't been since a shark took out a chunk of her leg. Almost died. We were all down in Mexico…" The surfer shakes his head. "She doesn't have enough strength in her leg."

"Whoa," says Charles. "That's quite a story." He checks his watch. "I gotta go. Nice talking with you."

"Yeah, you too. If you see Mary, she hangs out here sometimes when the surf's up, be careful. She's beautiful, but ew-whee! She's … she's, well shit, she's just nuts. If there was a murder, it was these damn rocks. Poor kid. She lost her brother, but we lost a good buddy. It's not as much fun surfing here now, getting an adrenaline high."

Charles parks his car farther down the lot, close to where he had been yesterday. It is just ten. He closes his eyes and thinks about what has transpired in the past twenty-four hours. Surrounding him is the beauty under the bridge, the sunlight, the colors, the sounds, the encounter with a beautiful woman. How will this story play out?

OHMMMMMMM. The fog is moving in, hiding the sun.

OHMMMMMMM. the horn sounds again. It is after eleven, almost high noon.

She isn't coming.

End of Story

THIN LINE BETWEEN

It's a thin line between bravery and stupidity. I'm now on that line, venturing along the razor's edge, a dangerous place to be with the two sides carefully balanced. Any mistake could lead to disaster.

The time is the late 1970s. The place: outside the Golden Gate. At first light, I'd sailed alone beneath the bridge on the ebb tide.

I was part of a group of sailors who planned a single-handed race around the Farallon Islands and back.

The islands are twenty-eight miles west of San Francisco, a challenging, but possible, sail. Guest speakers brought information to our meetings about coastal sailing and potential dangers, including single handing for long periods of time. We were given a list of required equipment for the race. The usual: food and water, foul weather gear, a compass and charts, and a marine radio. This was before cell phones. Radios were large, bulky, and expensive. I chose not to purchase one. I figured that if I was in such a dire situation that I needed help, I would be in no condition to use a radio. I trusted my boat and my sailing skills.

I'm sailing a Ranger 20, with a 500-pound keel and swing-down center board. It also has a self-bailing cockpit. Forward, in the cuddy cabin is a V-berth with a foam pad. Everything is stowed out of sight. Water, food, and all. Nothing will be loose, sliding around if it gets rough out there.

Sailing from my Sausalito moorage, I depart about an hour ahead of the racing fleet who launch from a marina on the east shore of San Francisco Bay. I turn west under the Golden Gate Bridge. I can hear the rumble of traffic above me on the rust-red span. The first of the incoming ocean swells gently lifts me. It's an exhilarating feeling. I'm excited. My body is vibrating. Off in the distance, out in the Pacific Ocean, a storm has blown itself out. Only the storm surge remains, arriving on the west coast as gently rolling waves. The weather forecast is for clear skies. The wind is strong, but manageable. I consider tucking in a reef on the mainsail but do not want to take the time.

My course is just outside, to the right, of the shipping lane. No departing freighter will surprise me from behind. This directs me through the Potato Patch, an area of known rough water. I've confronted this area before when I worked a season for a commercial fisherman. We used the small boat channel through the Patch to the north. The trough between the waves was often so deep that both the channel marker and the boat had to be on the top of a wave to make certain one was in the channel.

The sea is building. Soon I'll cross through and out of the Potato Patch. The Lightship Buoy is anchored ahead. I'm beyond the Patch and supposedly into the gentle ocean swells. But the waves continue to build, as well as the wind speed. I should have reefed. For the first time I begin to question my desire, my need to sail around the Farallons. Was it for bragging rights? Who else in my circle of friends has sailed that far out? Or do I need to prove something to myself? I don't know. I feel pretty comfortable in my own skin. There have been enough adventures in my thirty-eight years to last for a long time. Do I really need another?

My boat is solid. It's a new design but has proven to be safe and reliable. It has acquired a nickname, "Unsinkable Molly Brown," within the small boating world.

I have no desire to prove this.

This boat is my foundation, my security blanket, my support for the race out in the big ocean. My sails are set on an easy starboard tack, the wind is out of the northwest, hopefully all the way to the islands. The waves and wind increase, throwing me up the wall of approaching rushing water. Arriving at the crest, the sails, which had lost much of the wind in the trough, catch the gusts and slam over to the limit of their controlling sheet lines. The boat shudders, the rigging whipping. I am concerned for the deck stepped mast.

The wind gives the boat a kick, flinging it ahead over the crest and down into the trough behind the wave, just as the next wave rises to pound into the falling hull. BAMMM! The boat shudders again. And again, and again, wave after wave.

With each fall, the V-berth mattress floats in the air as the boat pitches down. My butt is getting sore from the repeated slamming. How much more of this punishment can my boat take? How much more can my body take?

At the top of the next wave, I look back towards the Golden Gate. We've come a long way. The powerful ebb tide has pushed us far out into the open ocean. The tidal current is also pushing against the wind, increasing the size and turbulence of the restless sea. The splash from the bow plunging into the next wave has soaked me, not a good way to start a long sail. Fortunately, my foul weather gear is keeping me warm. The increasing wind blows spray from the wave crests.

Some of the words from John Masefield's poem *Sea-Fever* come to mind.

I must go down to the seas again, …

…a clear call that may not be denied.

And the flung spray and the blown spume…

My memory lacks any more of the words, a research project for when I return.

Reality is staring me in the face. I've been sailing for about three hours, with a long day ahead. I'm getting tired, not good for future decision making. The wind's increasing. The height of the waves is increasing. Not a good combination. If the waves get steeper, my boat may stall on its forward motion up the surface. Or the bow may be plunged so deep in the next wave that momentum is lost as the hull struggles to throw off the burden of water. The boat must not end up sideways in the wave trough. I don't think my boat would roll over and capsize, but…

The realization that I am on the thin line has implanted itself in my thoughts. The line has become narrower and sharper. It is now the razor's edge. There is danger on both sides, ahead and behind. For whatever action is taken, or not taken, there's the potential for disaster. It's a difficult situation where any mistake may be very dangerous.

Somewhere along the line between bravery and stupidity, there must be rational thinking. It's time to go back. However, turning around in these conditions is not easy. I could gibe. Steering off the wind until it catches the sail on the other side. Sounds easy, but the wind would violently throw the sail over to the other tack as it fills. I've seen a boat lose its mast in a gibe, as the sail snaps to the other tack, the strain too great for the rigging.

Coming about is the only rational solution to my situation. But how and when? I could start my turn in the trench between waves, but I may not have enough wind down there to complete the turn. It would not be good to stall, with no forward movement for steering, with the next wave rapidly approaching.

The decision is made. I let two waves pass under me. I haven't been able to find a rhythm so have stopped looking for a smaller wave.

I feel in tune with my boat and the sea around me. Just before the crest of the next wave, I thrust the tiller over and slide my body to the other side of the cockpit. The boat swings into the eye of the wind. The bow comes around, much faster than I'd expected. I wait for just a moment to release the jib sheet. The jib backwinds with the wind on the wrong side of the sail. This moment, with the backwinded sail, results in two important consequences. The force on the back side of the sail pushes the bow around very quickly on the new tack. At the same time, the forward movement of the boat immediately slows, almost stopping. With no water moving past the rudder, the boat is out of control. The wave continues to roll up under the boat. We are almost at the crest, the stern swinging round to point at the approaching trough and the next wave. Everything's happening so fast, I don't have time to worry about getting "pooped," hitting the next wave stern first. It's a very dangerous position to be caught in. The back end of a boat is not designed to take the brunt of a wave.

I release the jib sheet, freeing the tortured sail to snap to the other side. A loop is thrown over the jib winch, the sheet pulled in. The wind fills the sails on the port tack, a broad reach. Perfect timing. The boat has spun around on the new tack so fast, we never descended into the trough between waves. We surf down the face of the wave, sailing faster than the following sea. With the combination of strong winds, the broad reach tack, and surfing, I actually have to slow the boat to keep from outrunning the following wave. It's easy to set my course across the waves to sail back home in the center of the shipping lane, thus avoiding returning through the Potato Patch. Sailing past, I can see the waves over in the Patch building up with rolling crests forming on their tops, a dangerous condition for a small boat.

Approaching the Golden Gate Bridge, the fleet of small racing boats passes me on their way west. I'm relieved to see that many skippers have already reefed their sails. They'll need them. For a moment, a very brief moment, I considered coming about and joining the group.

There's a disagreement as to how many boats took part in the Farallon Islands race, somewhere between thirty and sixty. Only fifteen completed the race, three made it back late the next morning, much to the relief of the race committee. There were reports of broken bones, suffered by skippers falling inside their boats in the rough seas, and a possible rescue by a Coast Guard helicopter.

When I returned to my moorage in Sausalito, I tied up and fell asleep in the forward V-berth, exhausted.

Choosing the bravery side of the thin line put a satisfying grin on my face. It was brave of me to admit my limitations, to turn around and head for home. Brave to accept that I will never brag about having sailed single-handed around the Farallon Islands.

STUFF

Stuff, STUFF, drawers stuffed with stuff. Where did it all come from? I'm not really a pack rat, but… everything here was important at the time… and still is. Maybe I should just leave it for someone else to deal with? Landfill? Pass it on? Naw, the grandkids have their own chests to stuff with their collections.

Here is a Kansas rattlesnake rattle. I had been plowing when there in front of me was a snake, coiled to fight off the approaching huge diesel tractor. It might be a "bullsnake," which looks like a rattlesnake without the rattle or venomous teeth. A good snake, they pray on jackrabbits, which eat the wheat.

The snake's rattle is now in my stuff drawer.

And on down through the layers, almost like an archeological dig. A scrimshaw pendant with an engraving of a bear cub on a bear's fang. From a trip to Alaska when my power animal was a bear. Another pendant with my birthstone, a sapphire. I was studying the psychic/spiritual powers of gemstones. My spirit guide often came to me in blue-ness. A key to the Marina Harbor moorage gate; my boat was there. Its name eludes me. Oh well, the good times and images are enough.

Keys, many keys. I have no idea what locks they fit. Important at the time, but now they go into metal recycling.

On the bottom, under a small envelope, are a few coins.

Mementoes of countries I've visited. Ceylon is no more. It's now Sri Lanka. I don't know what currency that country is using now. But when I pick up the old coin, the memories of that visit seventy years ago are vividly present. The marketplace, men selling goats and camels, not wanting their picture taken. The pungent smoke from incense lit at the feet of a giant Buddha, mixing with the odors of unwashed worshippers bowing before the statue.

On and on, country after country. What to do with these coins? Landfill? There's no monetary value, no silver or gold. Many are stamped from cheap aluminum. But the memories are priceless. My stuffed brain does not have to be sorted out, unlike my drawers.

Now, as I sort out, give away, and throw away my stuff, my brain is overflowing with memories. I am fortunate. My body does not work well, but my mind is filled with the accumulated wealth of a lifetime.

With some hesitation, I open the remaining envelope in the bottom of the drawer. A photo. I had forgotten it, so much has happened since. The picture of the beautiful young woman I had fallen love with fifty years ago. The smile on her face and the look in her eyes reflect back the deep mutual love we had.

We were both married.

Yet…

And yet.

Now, a lifetime later. (Why am I crying?)
I am "Grandpa" to her grandchildren.

ACKNOWLEDGEMENTS

I want to thank my friend, mentor, teacher, and editor Tim Crandle for his continued guidance and encouragement. You helped me channel my creativity into words, a priceless gift at this stage in my life.

Big sky thanks as well to my editor and writing coach Stacey Alysa Dennick who teased out the best version of every story in this book. In addition to cleaning up tenses, she prompted me to cut digressions and dive deeper into emotions. She didn't pressure, just offered suggestions for clarification, plot, or character development. It was a pleasure working with her on the cover and book interior design as well. I appreciate that she intuitively understands my non-linear, multi-dimensional reality, while bringing dedication and light-hearted humor to the long task of birthing a book.

ABOUT THE AUTHOR

Welton Rotz has been a sculptor of stone and metal, a blacksmith, licensed general contractor, boat builder and teacher. In the early 1960s he pursued graduate studies in Theology. Disenchanted with church doctrine, Welton did not complete his degree, preferring to develop his spirituality through meditation, extensive research, and creativity. He went on to study psychotherapy.

Born in 1940, Welton lived with relatives on a wheat and cattle farm for six months before moving to the Philippines with his college professor parents at the age of nine. After four years overseas, Welton returned to the states. He spent every summer during high school and college farming with his uncle and cousin in western Kansas. Sculpting and sailing have been his passion for many years.

In 2015 Welton was diagnosed with a rare, progressive amyloid neurological disease which severely impacted his hands and feet. He lives in San Francisco with his wife Barbara Stuart and an Icelandic sheepdog named Mikilee. There, he types stories with a stick held between his bent fingers.